A Short Walk in the Rain

Hugh Hood

A Short Walk in the Rain

THE COLLECTED STORIES

II

The Porcupine's Quill, Incorporated

CATALOGUING IN PUBLICATION DATA

Hood, Hugh, 1928-
  A short walk in the rain

ISBN 0-88984-134-9

I. Title.

PS8515.O49S46 1989   C813'.54   C89-093925-X
PR9199.3.H66S46 1989

Published by The Porcupine's Quill, Inc., 68 Main Street, Erin,
Ontario NOB ITO with financial assistance from the Canada
Council and the Ontario Arts Council.

Distributed by The University of Toronto Press,
5201 Dufferin Street, Downsview, Ontario M3H 5T8.

Cover is after a painting by Noreen Mallory.

Edited for the press by Doris Cowan.

Printed and bound by The Porcupine's Quill.
The stock is Zephyr laid, and the type, Galliard.

For David and Ann Leventhal
with love from Noreen and me

Uniform with this volume:

Hugh Hood: *The Collected Stories*

I: Flying a Red Kite

Contents

Author's Introduction

THE THIRTEEN STORIES collected here have never been published before. They were written between 1957 and 1961, and are the body of work which taught me the unlimited range of possibilities inherent in this great literary form. They display some clear influences but as I hope to show they end in an achieved freedom.

Quite a while after I wrote 'A Short Walk in the Rain' in January 1957, I noticed that its title was an exact metrical echo of 'The Old Man and the Sea,' an iamb, a single heavily-stressed syllable, and an anapest. The resemblance didn't exactly surprise me because I had been quite conscious as I wrote the story that the final action of *A Farewell to Arms* consisted of a short walk in the rain. Frederic Henry kisses the face of his dead lover but is unable to feel anything. 'It was like saying goodbye to a statue.' He walks back to the hotel in the rain. Hemingway's peculiar and overmastering achievement in my eyes was this fusion of clear simple exact phrasing, in the insistent rhythms of contemporary speech with all its repetitions and false starts, with intense and usually very discomforting feeling. 'I don't know. I don't know what I want to eat.' 'And the war went very badly.' 'Isn't it pretty to think so?' The laconic, even stoic, simplicity of the diction and syntax imposed a tremendous containing pressure on the feeling.

'A Short Walk in the Rain' was my first story. I have never revised it nor attempted to publish it after one or two early rejections. To revise it would be to edit one's firstborn, an unnatural action. The story was deeply attached to the work of a master, from whose practices one would not have wished to depart; revision might destroy feeling. Most North American fiction since the early 1920s situates itself under the downpour of Hemingway's rain, which falls alike upon Truman Capote and Elmore Leonard. It was raining on me when I sat down, just after New Year's thirty-one years ago, to write the stories which, I theorized, would group themselves around the novels I proposed to make the centre of my work. When I had a dozen

stories to circulate to editors I'd begin sending them on their
rounds; their publication would pave the way for acceptance of
my novels. Oddly enough, that's exactly how things worked
out.

So it was as natural to me as breathing to make my first story
an account of the slow approach to self-knowledge of a young
man, and to ensure that at the end of the story the young man
would still be imperfectly aware of the complexity and unpred-
ictability of human relationships. 'The whole thing was very
mixed up.' In that closing line I tried to deliver something of the
understated puzzlement, confusion and alarm of a man who has
lived in New York for several years, served the appointed hitch
in the peacetime army under the draft, and begun to rise in the
world. The story takes place over about eight years, from
Truman's second inaugural in early 1949 to a present day which
is approximately the time of writing, 1957, when the narrator is
in his late twenties, still frightened and confused and mixed up.
It's a longish story. As I examine it in the light of long experience I judge that it isn't a short story at all; it contains the material of a long story, perhaps even a novella, and I see that I have
had to compress, to fudge, to move rapidly over events which
should have taken longer in the telling. The narrator is con-
fronted with a group of family relations among Italian Americans which are subtle and widely ramified, at the centre of which
the figure of the mother should take the most honoured place.
Reading the story now, I become sharply aware that the
unnamed and obscure relatives who shift the care of Mama onto
Bella and Angelo are probably Mafiosi.

My narrator suspects nothing of these complexities; he is
preoccupied with finding his way in the enormous metropolis,
and he is perfectly trustworthy only so far as he is reporting
observations and facts. He doesn't even guess that Angelo and
Bella aren't husband and wife but brother and sister until he is
asked to witness a will. There are several levels of partial aware-
ness involved here. If the narrator is so impercipient about the
world around him how can he understand himself? Is he in any
sense competent to report anything? I think that he is trustworthy but incompetent, as it were. He believes himself to be
speaking the truth, but frankly admits at the end of his narrative

that he doesn't understand much of what happens to him. *The whole thing* is mixed up, not just the affair of the location of Mama's burial plot.

I meant then, as I mean now, that the story was chiefly interesting as a narrative contrivance. Ostensibly it has two tales to tell, that of the Mazzaferros' mysterious family relations and their worship and service of Mama, and that of the gradual maturing of the narrator. The effect of the story should lie in the pattern formed by the adjustment of the two story lines as counterpoised to one another; the art lies in the juxtaposition. I don't think that the story as it stands is perfect, but I consider it a success and would never lay a revisionist hand on it. I learned an immense amount in writing 'A Short Walk in the Rain'. I remember sitting back in my chair when I wrote the closing lines and heaving an amazed sigh, saying to myself exultingly, 'Look what you can do with these things! Think of the possibilities!' And I started immediately on a second story, 'A Faithful Lover', which was written in the second half of January 1957. Two stories in a month!

Perhaps I should say something about the pace at which I have usually written my stories. This is a matter of wide disagreement among writers. Scott Fitzgerald could write a commercial story in two, or at most three, writing sessions. We don't always know how long these sessions were. Then he would allow himself a day or two for minor revision and retyping, 'and off she goes.' The inside of a week seems to have sufficed in most instances. We must remember that he usually worked under the pressure of immediate financial necessity.

I've almost never been able to produce a story that fast; for one thing, I almost never write a story that I haven't been thinking over for a long time, sometimes as long as thirty years ('Breaking Off'), and rarely as short a time as a few months ('Deanna and the Ayatollah'). I prepare a story in my head, in a long process of mulling over and recasting. I virtually never get an idea and write it up at once. But when the basic idea has been marinated, so to speak, I usually complete the first draft in five days, then put the text aside for a couple of weeks to allow for second and third thoughts. Ordinarily I'll pencil in fairly substantial verbal adjustments to my text, though rarely any extensive addition or excision; that sort of editing has already been done mentally. The final draft is usually the work of a further five or six days of typing. From first to last I can write the story comfortably in a month. I once wrote a story a month for fourteen months and published them all.

Occasionally I've written faster than that. In 1966 I wanted to produce the collection *Around the Mountain: Scenes From Montréal Life* rather quickly, so that the book could conveniently be issued early in Expo year. I made a careful outline, then wrote two stories a month for six months, January / June 1966, including revisions and final polishing. I met my self-imposed deadline but I wouldn't attempt the same feat again.

In the summer of 1960 I wrote five stories in the space of five weeks – just about Fitzgerald's pace – and the results were varied and interesting. One story was a grand success which has been widely admired; another which has never been published until now seems to me a purely derivative story which works very well in its model's terms; a third had a remarkable subsequent career in the form of a play for network television; the fourth was an anecdote told to me by my sister-in-law (I simply wrote down what she told me, making minor editings for the sake of patterning); the fifth is plainly an artistic nullity. In the order described, the stories were: 'The Chess Match', 'The Regulars', 'Friends and Relations', 'A Childhood Incident', and 'High Fidelity'. The best and the worst of them were both completely invented stories without any anecdotal base. The three middling ones were rooted in observed experience. You simply never know what you may get when you begin to write, especially when you're working fast. Those five were written for *Esquire* to consider. None of them was accepted there, a lesson of some kind. In the end, they've all seen the light of day, two of them in the present collection. I would be unable to write a story a week these days, not from lack of energy or invention, but because I would see too far into the possibilities of the *donnée*, would be unable to leave it alone after a single week.

'A Faithful Lover', my second story, is a case in point. As I read it over in the late 1980s, I'm almost irresistibly impelled to rewrite it, because I can see so many elements in it which I might have developed further or better. But I've always declined to tinker with finished stories long after they've been completed, as Henry James did with his early novels when he edited his collected works towards the end of his life. I'm on Beethoven's side; he refused to impose the refinements of his late style on early work given to the public long after its composition. My position has been that I wrote each story as well as I could within the limitations of the resources and insight I possessed at the time of writing; later correction would inevitably throw out of kilter the subtle inner relationships of the original version of the text. Three times I have made some light, copyeditor's revisions to stories, but I've never completely revised one or altered the line of the narration.

I can see these days that few readers will accept the fundamental premise of 'A Faithful Lover' as credible. A young man, with a history of emotional disturbance and an intense religious life, believes implicitly and naïvely in the Catholic doctrine concerning the sacraments, especially that concerning the cleansing and saving action of baptism. He persuades his fiancée to follow a course of religious instruction culminating with reception of the three sacraments traditionally bestowed at the end of such a course, baptism, followed by penance and reception of the Eucharist. The young woman is now in a perfectly regenerate state of grace and innocence, without any stain of guilt on her soul. He kills her, acting on his conviction that her soul will go immediately to Heaven.

I've never published this story, nor tried more than once or twice to place it in a magazine, because I suspected that such an action could not be rendered credible to the contemporary secular mind. Was I right? I still don't know. My models were the theological novels of Graham Greene, *Brighton Rock, The End of the Affair*, and especially *The Heart of the Matter*, still perhaps Greene's most celebrated work. Major Scobie, a thoroughly convinced believer, knows himself to be in a state of mortal sin and that receiving Holy Communion prior to a good confession means damnation, an eternity of torment. Scobie feels an enormous pity for his wife, whom he has consistently lied to and betrayed sexually; he cannot bear to undeceive her about their relations. At the same time he persuades himself that he is unable to confess his sins and be forgiven. He knowingly receives the Blessed Sacrament while in a state of mortal sin, to reassure his wife that he is in his ordinary, normal state of behaviour, that nothing is wrong between them. In doing this he risks damnation to ensure the peace and tranquillity of another. Not long afterwards he dies. We are left with the unresolvable puzzle about what will happen to him in eternity. To me, a believing Catholic then and now, this story is fascinating, and I have obviously tried to propose a similar riddle in my story. What will happen to John Carroll? Execution? A lifetime in a psychiatric ward? Terrible suffering in any case. Murder is a mortal, damning, sin.

This narrative is probably only manageable in a novel by a much more experienced writer. The story did, however, allow me to introduce the invisible agencies of supernatural grace, the Redemption and Atonement of Christ, liturgical prayer, the action of contemplation, into a fiction, much as Greene and François Mauriac had done in their exemplary work. I still don't know enough to write this story, and I've never written another even remotely like it.

The following month I did write a more successful story about the religious life, 'Cura Pastoralis', but it was in no sense a theological romance in the manner of Greene. I turned towards the world of social appearances and traceable motives in my next few attempts, including a pair of stories which might now be seen as Bakhtinian in form. They seem to follow the principles of polyphonic fiction proposed by M.M. Bakhtin in his work on Dostoevsky and Rabelais. Character, the person, never constructs itself in isolation but invariably in close, symbiotic confrontation with another or others. The human person has no true existence apart from others. In 'The Strategies of Hysteria', February 1957, I thought that I was attempting a sharp social satire by delivering a rude snapshot of Mrs. J. Delta Williams, a personage closely modelled upon a certain landlady of mine in West Hartford. I was preparing to leave her home, where I'd never been really comfortable. I'm not really proud of having written this story, which treats its model unkindly.

I got married, and Noreen and I moved into an apartment in another part of the city. In the summer of 1957 I began to feel uneasy about my portrait of Mrs. J. Delta Williams. She was generating herself polyphonically in my mind, to use Bakhtin's terminology. Several months later I found myself obliged to write 'That 1950 Ford' in which my original narrator – not far from my own voice and angle of judgement – meets a bizarre and arbitrary end as 'the late Mr. Twombley'. Mrs. Williams and Mr. Twombley are equally perplexed about goings-on in West Hartford. The blindnesses of one character give rise to perceptions in others; their perplexities in turn compel his or her certainties. 'That 1950 Ford' was one of the few stories I revised lightly some time later. I'm still not too happy with it.

By now I'd written half a dozen stories, two of which were afterwards to be among my first publications. I was falling more and more deeply in love with the formal opportunities of the medium. I now arrived at a fundamental resolution about technique. I would make it a rule never to tell the same story twice, and never to employ the same rhetorical structure too often. I had no objection to imitating another writer's work, however, especially if his or her story seemed to open the door to valuable experiment. I've never rejected 'influences'. The next two stories I wrote, towards the end of 1957, were formal experiments, and one was almost – not quite – a plagiarism. I loved the stories in Ray Bradbury's *The Illustrated Man*, particularly because of their introduction of moral and religious reflection and instruction in the guise of science fiction. It was a commonplace at the time that Ray Bradbury wasn't really writing science fiction, just something that looked a bit like it. This authorial strategy pleased and intrigued me. As anyone who has read both stories sees immediately, 'The World By Instalments' is a reworking of Bradbury's fascinating story 'The Veld' from *The Illustrated Man*.

Chaucer and Shakespeare don't hesitate to retell stories by their predecessors; this is a licence traditionally granted to storytellers. I felt that I was introducing a valuable modification of Bradbury's story. Both narratives start with the idea that a family home can be furnished with enormous television screens on all four walls. Once in place these screens allow the family, or any of its members, to create imagined lives in which they can act as real participants. In Ray Bradbury's story, the children combine to create a dangerous life on the African veld, complete with ravenous wild beasts. They then persuade their parents into this imaginary but wholly real world and trap them there, abandoning them to the mercies of lions. It is a story of children against parents. My rearrangement of the fundamental idea was to introduce a strong erotic element, making it a story of mother and son against father and daughter. Mary Thorne and her son Bobby escape into the imaginary world of the walls because of the intensity of their fantasy lives and their incestuous relationship. Abe Thorne and his daughter Jean are left behind to share one another's bald world of ordinary reality.

I remember deciding to use a Jamesian turn of phrase at carefully selected points in the story, to qualify the alien and futuristic conception of the walls and the oddity of the language of this future world (*sod-o-mat, solar nutrient, glassola*). This was an unfortunate decision; the Jamesian tone refuses to merge with the children's dialogue. The narrative line has ugly and even shocking implications not found in Bradbury's original, but the story remains an unsatisfactory essay in the mode of allegory disguised as science fiction. I have never since attempted that mode.

'The Glass of Fashion', on the other hand, is an early and uncertain glance towards a kind of story I have often attempted since, which I call 'media folklore'. Our lives began to be dominated to an extraordinary extent, during the 1950s and 1960s, the age of Marshall McLuhan, by the influence of the media. *Understanding Media* could have been the title of any book written at that time. It could certainly have been the title of 'The Glass of Fashion'. My Shakespearian choice of title proposes an oblique comment on the nature of the dramatic and histrionic and their effect on communication.

Porky Valentine bears the first of those emblematic names that a long line of my characters have worn: Arthur Merlin, Rose Leclair, Matthew Goderich. He is treated as an element in a typological exemplum, not as a character in a short story. Any personage in fiction whose name is Valentine trails a long chain of associations behind him of love and romance; these are somewhat mitigated by the unromantic 'Porky'.

'The Glass of Fashion' is then a media folk-tale; it resembles traditional folk-tales in its journey motif, and in the surprising transformations of the various settings into their opposites. The deep woods of northwestern Connecticut turn into a haven for admen and magazine editors. The Canadian wilderness is suddenly changed into a campground for drunken tourists; there is a strong flavour of the magically revelatory about the story. Three 'Yale men' get together for cocktails and it turns out that one went to Saint Lawrence University, another to Georgetown, and the third to the University of Akron! Porky finds increasingly that nothing is what it seems; the media world is an enchanted and invented world and one invention succeeds another with dreadful speed. There is a flavour of Spenser's Cave of Mammon.

When Porky undertakes a final magical transformation of himself into a simple, innocent, frank and manly son of the wilderness – a story which John Buchan might have told without any qualification – he finds that some grand general overriding purpose in and of the media world has realigned and altered all his associates in the same way. You might call this Fate or Destiny, or just The Media. I'm still quite pleased with 'The Glass of Fashion'. I can see in it many aspects of narration which were to become prominent in my work when once I'd found my own line. That was the last story I wrote in 1957, my first year in the game, and it seemed an encouraging omen. Some of the 'media folklore' conceptions embedded in 'Fallings From Us, Vanishings', 'O Happy Melodist!', 'Crosby', 'Doubles' and 'None Genuine Without This Signature' had already lifted themselves above the horizon.

I didn't write any more stories for several months. I was finishing up my first, unpublished novel, *God Rest You Merry*, which was completed in the spring of 1958. In April our first child, Sarah, was born. She immediately began to thrust her way into my fiction, appearing almost as herself in 'After the Sirens', 'Flying a Red Kite', and 'Nobody's Going Anywhere', three stories in my first book. Long before it was published, Sarah – at about eight months – had manifested herself *en travesti* as young Tommy Megaffin in 'The Triumph of the Liturgy'.

Excitement about a first novel, and the early stages of enchanted parenthood, seem to have turned me away from the intricate strains of experiment in story form. Neither 'Marriage 401', November 1958, nor 'The Triumph of the Liturgy', December 1958, shows any interesting formal aspect. What remains worthy of discussion in these two minor stories is their vivid portrayal of two great social institutions as they were at that time, the university and the church. Neither institution has been at all the same since the 1960s. In 'Marriage 401' we meet a group of young university actors at a large Catholic university. Their behaviour is so unlike what their children do in the late 1980s that I find myself appalled in trying to understand the differences. I seldom write explicitly about sexual customs, and I am charmed, and rather alarmed, to find that the most offensive, deliberately gross reference that my young man can think of, with which to assault his girl-friend's defences, is to remark that he would love to kiss her bum! His sexual naïvety is overwhelming. The story may be compared with a much later one, 'Quicker Coming Back' in the collection *August Nights*. The later story is obsessively concerned with the double question of what you can and can't do, sexually, and what you can and can't say about what you do. I wanted 'Quicker Coming Back' to move towards the condition of pornography, and apparently it did so. Some of its readers have found it quite sufficiently stimulating. 'Marriage 401' isn't like that at all. Its innocence is overpowering, agreeable to those who enjoy innocence, repellent perhaps to those who don't.

'The Triumph of the Liturgy', written right at the end of 1958 when Eisenhower was president, Sputnik a top news story, Elvis Presley a threat to decency, shows its date of composition with utter clarity in its depiction of the great, assured, immovable American Catholic Church as it then existed in the northeastern U.S., as a massive presence in American post-industrial society, where priests routinely described the church, rectory, school, nuns' residence, collectively as 'the plant'. Eight masses on Sundays, all packed, with no nonsense about use of the vernacular in the liturgical text, with the Eucharist handed out casually at immense speed to long lines of communicants, with highly satisfactory offertories rolling in! The American Catholic Church – like the Church in Québec – seemed able in 1958 to withstand any imaginable assault.

Thirty years afterwards all that immense assurance has been swept away as though it had never existed. Only a few traces like 'The Triumph of the Liturgy' remain to show it as it was in its heyday. As a believing Catholic I remain fully persuaded that the gates of Hell will not prevail against Christ's foundation. I don't mourn for the excrescences stripped from the Church by thirty years of constant change. I don't mourn for 'the plant' and the huge inert congregations. I think that the vacant and the vain have been shaken out of the Church, which has often in its history been in a minority position and is probably better off in that position than as one of the great seats of ascendant power. I would remain in the Church and practise my faith if there were only a hundred of us left, or ten, or five.

A young Maryknoll missionary refuses to fit his mass to the customary pace and style of a parish's liturgical observances. The pastor doesn't like this, but when he finds collections increased by the procedure he 'is made most seriously to reflect.' That's all I hoped for from the story, a mild satiric sting, and that's about what I got. Otherwise, 'The Triumph of the Liturgy' is noteworthy only for its use of the present tense in a mode of report that was popularized by Tom Wolfe in the mid-1960s and has continued to be used by provincial journalists until the present. I haven't used the present tense for narration very often; it's a stylistic tic that I find boring.

My next two attempts at the story show an increasing command of the formal properties of the genre. 'Which the Tigress, Which the Lamb?' was meant to be a satiric fantasy owing something to Blake's 'Marriage of Heaven and Hell'. Blake always sees reality as deeply divided in dialectical opposition, tiger and lamb, innocence and experience. The question remains, which is innocent, the lamb or the tiger, which is experienced?

A mousy little woman student suddenly transforms herself into a contestant in the Miss America Pageant 'at famed Atlantic City.' In which role is she the tiger? I wish I knew. It is fascinating to me to recall that the final text of the story, from my rewriting of 1964, doesn't fit my original sense of the story's inner coherence. I wrote it in April 1959, when I was teaching at a women's college in Connecticut, where any such transformation would have caused immense concern, even distress, among the Sisters of Mercy who directed the institution. When I reset the story in Ontario, introducing references to Wentworth County, Toronto, Kingston, other familiar spots, the texture of the piece became blurred. A beauty pageant in southern Ontario simply doesn't have the same comic or satiric implications as in Connecticut or New Jersey in 1959 or in 1988. The point of the satire is blunted by the shift, and the text as it stands seems itchily uneasy. I only once more revised a story long after I'd completed it, and in that case similar damage was not inflicted.

'Presents for an Anniversary', from May 1959, attempts less than 'Which the Tigress, Which the Lamb?', but what is attempted is, I believe, modestly achieved. I still like the dialogue in the story, especially the exchanges between the two little sisters, Maddy and Kath, which strike me as accurate and convincing without being too cutesey-pooh. I didn't want them to sound like clever young actresses on some TV show, and I don't think that they do. The opening pages of this brief piece move very briskly; much is delivered about the relations between the girls and their baby sister and their parents. When we become able to judge the reality of their parents' dissatisfaction with one another, the implications of the opening exchange shift into a new perspective – which tells the story for me – so that the closing lines have considerable poignancy. Maddy is perfectly correct in her guess. Her mother really is planning to surprise her, but not in the way she expects.

I could have arranged this story so as to exclude the sideline witnesses, Paula and Joe, the childless couple who live in the same apartment building. In that case I'd have had to allow the children's mother to confess the family plight directly to her daughters, and the story would have veered towards a quality of pathos not justified by the material. I wanted the carefully managed alteration of tone in the opening and closing dialogues, and I believe I got it. 'Presents for an Anniversary' seems to me among the unpretentious successes of this collection.

For the record, the other successful attempts seem to me to be 'A Short Walk in the Rain', 'The Glass of Fashion', 'The Triumph of the Liturgy', 'The Regulars', and 'From the Fields of

Sleep'. Two of the others might qualify as interesting failed tries, 'A Faithful Lover' and 'The World By Instalments'. And then there are the stories which didn't succeed, whose original ideas weren't strong enough or whose narrative layout required more subtlety and ingenuity than I could supply. Nobody expects a ballplayer to hit the ball out of the park every time he comes to bat. I think that alert and generous readers are just as forgiving in this respect, so I won't apologize for including these five in the collection because I think it can often help the artist enormously to fail in an attempt. His or her failures may be even more instructive than the great successes. Mozart has plenty of dull works, and dull passages in successful works – the middle movement of the 'Prague' symphony may serve as an example – and our understanding of Mozart is enhanced by this discovery. Nobody's perfect. One of Haydn's symphonies has a first movement without a musical idea in it. I leave you to find which one!

I'd call stories like 'The Strategies of Hysteria', 'That 1950 Ford', 'Marriage 401', 'Which the Tigress, Which the Lamb?' and 'High Fidelity', instructive artistic failures. I might have done better with some of them if I'd attempted them later on. I wouldn't, however, try to salvage 'High Fidelity', poor thing. I feel as though I am betraying a once-loved infant by that admission. You have to love the idea of the story to begin writing it. I thought my title made a sly joke about married couples and their decisions to stay together or to part; but the joke wasn't very clever. I imagined that it was fresh and original to tell the story from the point of view of the cleaning lady, Mrs. Garvey, a method quite like that of 'A Short Walk in the Rain', but I could do little with Mrs. Garvey, who shows us nothing interesting about herself or her clients. The story retains only the interest of a failure of both method and idea.

'The Regulars' was written a month after 'High Fidelity', in July 1960, as one of five stories written in a five-week stretch at that period. While 'High Fidelity' came to grief, 'The Regulars', told in a very similar way, achieved a success of a peculiar kind. The narrator is quite fully characterized by his words and his tone. He is one of a group of men 'in the neighbourhood' who go to Dante D'Imonte's bar and grill every Friday and Saturday night, treating the place as their club, with certain powerful unspoken rules and customs.

> There are twenty to twenty-five of us who come in on both Friday and Saturday nights all the year round except during holiday time in the summer. We all know each other. Most of the guys have seen each other almost every day since they were kids going to Saint Clare's or Whitney Public.... Everybody's a Democrat.

The narrator and his friends are perfectly aware how much their group means to them. The story portrays the Irish and Italian Catholic, urban male group, which John O'Hara wrote about so angrily. His five or six big collections of stories in the 1960s include several stories very much like 'The Regulars': same length, same language, same use of status indicators to fix and identify different urban types. My narrator's self-awareness, his intense concern about who belongs to the group and who doesn't, are pure O'Hara. He doesn't like Bodza Mulhearne who 'squeezes in between two or three of the regulars and acts like he belongs, and in a way he does.' He sees Bodza as a marginal member of the group, and is uncertain about his own status among his peers. We identify him as the kind of man who, if three are walking down the street, never walks in the middle. When Bodza harasses a young stranger who intrudes on the group's privacy, the narrator knows that the little cab driver is behaving badly, that he couldn't get away with it without group solidarity at his back. But – and this is the point of the story – the narrator will back somebody he knows against a stranger every time, and he knows this about himself. Since Bodza chased somebody out of Dante's place, 'he's got a reputation. In a way he's more of a regular than ever before.' We can see the narrator getting quite pally with little Bodza.

That's a much better story than 'High Fidelity' and much better told, but I feel about it as a ventriloquist's dummy might be imagined to feel about his part in the act. I've delivered a perfect small John O'Hara story through my own voice-box.

A year went by during which I prepared to move back to

Canada. In early 1961 I began to write stories that have since become very widely known. By March 1961, in 'Fallings From Us, Vanishings', I was writing in what has become my own voice and manner. No more acts of ventriloquism. I don't think I've written a really derivative story since 'The Regulars'.

By the summer of 1961 we were comfortably located in our new home in Montréal. Our son Dwight had been born in April. When we got to Montréal I immediately wrote a sort of memoir about Dwight's arrival on the scene called 'Notes on Becoming a Father', and in July 1961 I wrote one of my best-known stories, 'Flying a Red Kite'. I don't think anybody would call it a derivative story or an apprentice piece. I'd managed, quite largely by writing the stories collected here, to get to the point where I could write accomplished fiction in my own style.

There was one unpublished story to come. A couple of weeks after I wrote 'Flying a Red Kite' I started the last one in this book, 'From the Fields of Sleep', which I revised lightly many years later. The revisions were trivial, and the story is published for the first time here, substantially as I wrote it in August 1961. I find it fascinating to think that 'Flying a Red Kite' should have received the warm welcome it has, all over the world, while a sister-story, written immediately afterwards, has never been published until now.

'From the Fields of Sleep' has all my trademarks: title from the 'Immortality' Ode, insistent use of bright colour imagery, a use of indirect free style which hovers between the first and third person, allowing the narrative to move from objective mimetic description to something pretty close to interior monologue, and the 'last survivor' story line I'd already used in 'After the Sirens'. There is a strong focus on detail presented with hallucinatory exactness in a magic-realist mode of perceiving. There is the fascination with death and dying and the gradual emergence from terror through hope to final exhilaration. There is the fascination with the narrative methods of the movies.

The principal source for 'From the Fields of Sleep' was the movie *Wake Island*, a glossy Paramount production featuring a strong cast of Paramount contract players, Brian Donlevy, William Bendix, Robert Preston, many other familiar studio figures. When I saw *Wake Island* on its release in 1942, I was fascinated by the inexorable advance of the invading Japanese forces, and by the fact that all the defenders would either be killed or taken prisoner; they had no possible way to escape. I often tried to imagine what I would do in that predicament.

All my life I have striven to make the very best possible of adversity. There is a sense, of course, in which human circumstances are always and finally adverse; we all lose the game in the end. Deep in the recesses of human nature lies the conviction that however diligent, however courageous, however farsighted we are, we can't defend ourselves against the overwhelmingly powerful invader of this island from which there can only be one escape route. I wanted to make 'From the Fields of Sleep' a testament to the supernatural virtue of hope, which I believe to be humanity's most valuable resource. Johnson, in 'From the Fields of Sleep', is much in Ishmael's position at the end of *Moby Dick*, that of the sole surviving witness.

There is a more proximate parallel, that with the plight of the central character in Hemingway's magnificent story 'The Snows of Kilimanjaro'. But my man Johnson is striving to escape from the hypnotic fascination of death and the wish for extinction which he shares with Hemingway's writer / hunter. Both stories end with an ascent in an aeroplane towards a high wide prospect of light, but Hemingway's character is dying – is perhaps already dead – of the effects of a putrefying gangrene. Johnson isn't dead. He refuses to contemplate the prospect of death.

> He might make friendly waters; when he came down there might be a chance to be picked up, maybe he would get home, you never can tell. But it all depended on him and his luck. It didn't depend on the enemy or anybody else.
>
> He came back slowly on the stick. And as the bright red eye of day, the sun in the blue, went up the sky, and the bands of clouds parted in the east, he felt the drive and lift of the river of air under him, and he

rose with and into the red sun, alone, absolutely unconditioned by men, and free.

Free.

In 'Flying a Red Kite', that same river of air was blowing across the top of the mountain in Montréal 'in a steady uneddying stream'. It is the breath of life, the movement of the Spirit which liberates us from the overwhelming invader and, precisely, makes us free.

Hugh Hood
January 1988

A Short Walk in the Rain

A Short Walk in the Rain

I ARRIVED IN NEW YORK a week before Truman's second inaugural and got a job in the mailroom at *Time*. They were desperate for help and put me to work immediately. For ten days I shuttled back and forth between New York and Washington, carrying instructions and photographic supplies to staffers on the inaugural story, and bringing back plates to be developed. All that time I averaged four hours' sleep a night between flights. I stayed mostly at YMCAs and made some money on my expenses.

I hadn't time to look for a place to live at first but when things quieted down I discovered that the Y kept a list of rooming houses which it approved. I asked for some leads and they listed five cheap locations for me. I picked the first one on the list and went down to see about it as soon as I had some free time.

It was on West 24th Street, over past Eighth Avenue. As I looked at it from the street, I knew that it must be inexpensive. It was a five-storey apartment tenement without an elevator and, of course, I'd been directed to Apartment 5-A, four double flights of stairs to climb every day. That was the only exercise I got for the next couple of years. And I remember hoping that I was really getting the feel of New York at last. 'Living all the way downtown,' I thought, 'right in the middle of a slum. Very romantic.' I was pretty naïve.

And I was wrong about it's being a slum because at the end of the block there were three apartments that had been done over and were renting for eight thousand a year. You get that kind of situation downtown – tenements and delicatessens and dry-cleaners – and then these wonderful remodelling jobs. One thing was, it was right next to the Eighth Avenue subway.

So I started to climb. On the fourth floor landing, a tall raw-boned Irishwoman of seventy with a purple face and mad eyes bounded out of a door, past me, and down the stairs like a ton of coal. We never spoke, all the time I stayed there, but I used to see her on the stairs and in church on 14th Street. At first I thought she was really out of her mind because she talked to herself all the time. Much later I realized that she was reciting her beads. I listened to her slam the door away below me. Then the building was quiet again and I went up the last flight.

When I knocked at Apartment 5-A, Bella answered the door. She was the shortest woman I'd ever seen who wasn't a dwarf; she couldn't have been more than four foot six. She wasn't delicately built; she had a big head with a lot of frizzy brownish-grey hair and a pair of round enormous eyes. She stared at me out of the darkness, rather frightening me, although as things turned out I had no reason to be afraid. She made a growling noise in her throat and I stared at her dumbly. Up the hall behind her somebody moved and I could have sworn I heard a groan.

'You want to see me?' she said. Then she swayed, or rather lurched, around, pushing the door open. 'Come in,' she said. When she moved, I saw that she had an enormous brace – it had four thick metal clasps – on her right leg. She always walked at an acute angle and at about one mile an hour; the brace must have weighed forty pounds.

'Come in,' she said again and I walked silently up the hall, feeling foolish for some reason, perhaps because I could walk so much easier than she could. Anyway we went into the kitchen and she gave me a chair. Before I could say anything else, she started moving painfully around, getting things out of cupboards. She put a coffee ring, with raisins and nuts in it, on the table, a cake, and a bottle of wine, and then she started to make coffee, all without saying a word.

When the coffee was ready she poured me a cup, indicated the cream and sugar with a twist of her neck, and left the room. From another part of the apartment I heard a long string of high-pitched excited Italian, an old lady's voice. I began to drink the coffee, trying to follow the conversation, but it was no use; it came too fast. All I could get was the notion that the old lady was quite irritated about something. Then I noticed that the coffee I was drinking was strong enough to take the top of my head off. I put some cold water in it as quietly as I could, sat back, and waited.

In a minute Bella inched her way back into the kitchen, folded her arms across her chest, and stood watching me as I finished the coffee. Even watered down it was making me shudder.

'Another cup?'

'Well,' I said, 'I don't really think I ...'

'Come on. Come on. We got lots. Have some cake and another cup.' I wondered if this was some new kind of sales pitch but I couldn't refuse. She was always giving people things. In a few days I realized that nobody would ever refuse to take things from her. I drank another cup and began to feel violently over-stimulated. It struck me that I ought to say who I was and why I was there so I fumbled in my pocket and found my list.

'I heard you had a room to rent,' I said. 'I just came to New York and I need a place to live. I don't know anybody in town but the YMCA sent me to you.'

'We got a room,' she said. 'Do you want to look at it?'

'If you're not too busy.'

'I got all day,' she said, smiling. 'Come along the hall; it's by the door.'

It was no different from the kind of room I'd have found in Toronto. There was a good bed, a chest of drawers, a table and a great big red-and-gold picture of the Sacred Heart. Everything was clean. Usually in these old apartments in the city there's a lot of dust but this room was surprisingly clean. The closet was too small but I only had two suits anyway so that was all right. Bella could see that I was pleased, I guess, because she began to act right away as if I'd lived there for years.

'Where do you work?' she wanted to know. I told her that I was with *Time*, Inc. and she seemed impressed.

'Maybe you write something about me and Angelo?'

'I only work for the business department.'

'Later on, then.' She never got it through her head that I was just a guy in the mailroom. The questions she asked, you'd have thought I was our Paris correspondent. She was fascinated when I told her about my trips back and forth to Washington.

'Did you just get back?'

'Yes. I've got to go out again to-night.'

'On an aeroplane?'

'Yes.'

'Wonderful. I wish I could go. I haven't been out for years –

on account of the stairs. I don't climb so good.'

'What do you do for sunlight?'

'Fire escape. I get a good view from there.'

I didn't believe that she stayed in all the time. It was true, though. In the two years I was there she was out once. Not more than twice. And then, there was Mama.

When I told Bella that I'd take the room, nine dollars a week with breakfast, and that I'd bring my bag down when I got back from Washington, she led me back to the kitchen, poured me another cup of her lethal coffee, and told me all about Mama and Angelo.

'The relatives give us something to help with Mama and we take care of her. She's old and she doesn't see too good and she can't speak much English. Maybe you can learn some Italian.'

'I'd love to.'

'You'll have to, if you want to be comfortable here. Mama hates English and she hates strangers.'

'Was it me she sounded so mad about?'

'Yes; but she's always mad about something. You'll see.'

It took about six months for Mama to thaw out because she really was afraid of any kind of change. After I learned a little Italian, things went along better. She used to tell me all about the country around Brescia and Lake Garda and about how much she hated New York. She was a cranky old soul, not the lovable Granny type at all, and I often wondered why they put up with her; she did nothing but complain and the other relatives wouldn't have her in the house. I suppose Angelo and Bella, being so nice, were the natural-born fall-guys in the family.

Bella was the nearest thing to a real saint I ever saw. Sometimes when my parents or my brother were in the city I'd have them come up to visit and they got the same impression. Bella was a terrific personage and Angelo was just the same. He was a tiny little guy, very neatly made, very pleasant, who worked for the Post Office. He'd have all these different shifts; God alone knows who arranges the hours in the Post Office. We used to sit around the kitchen talking things over for hours, especially civil service salary regulations. Angelo didn't make much money and at that time neither did I so we used to complain to each other how ill-treated we were, the way guys do in the army. It wasn't very serious.

'Got a split-shift for the next month,' he'd grumble. 'Four hours on, then a four-hour break, then another four hours. I'm really working twelve hours with no overtime.'

'One thing about my job,' I'd say to tease him. 'Lots of overtime.' I was making more than he was even then.

When I'd been with *Time*, Inc. eighteen months I got a chance to join their executive training program. My basic salary was nearly doubled and I began to think about sharing an apartment with another guy at work. We looked around for a month or two, found one, arranged for some furniture, and I left Angelo and Bella's place after I'd been with them almost exactly two years. The last few days I was there, I felt terrible about leaving, much more than I'd expected. They were the first people I'd known in New York and they had been very kind to me. I tried to make it plain to them that I wanted to keep up the association.

After that I used to go down to see them once a month and they always had coffee and cake or a drink to offer me. I was always glad to see them and glad to get away. After all, I mean, we weren't living in the same atmosphere. In the training program I was meeting some of the top men in the company although I myself had no particular status except that of a more or less bright young man. Then all at once things changed. I got drafted. I didn't have to go because I wasn't a citizen at the time but I figured, what the hell, I'm earning my living here. The company couldn't give me a permanent appointment in any department until I got back.

The first weeks were tough. Two years seemed like a lifetime – as though everything I'd been working for was irretrievably out of reach. We couldn't leave the post and nobody came to see me, at least, nobody from the office. I felt miserable. Then, one Saturday afternoon, who should appear but old Angelo! He'd come forty miles across Jersey after leaving work at eight in the morning. He was the first person who had taken the trouble. I nearly cried; I was never so glad to see anybody in my life.

'I'm on the midnight shift, twelve to eight,' he said. 'Lots of overtime.'

'There's plenty of overtime on this job,' I said. 'But I'm not getting paid for it.'

'You running a little short?'

'Insurance and furniture payments,' I said. 'I haven't got a dime.'

'I brought you some cigarettes,' he said, handing them over. 'And candy, here.'

We talked a blue streak for a couple of hours until he had to go. By the time he got home and into bed, I figured, it would be five-thirty or six. I asked him about Bella and the Post Office and Mama.

'Mama isn't so good. She's showing her age,' he said.

'Let me know how things come out. Remember me to everybody on the block, and come back any time, really, I mean it. Any time.'

He promised he would. When he left me at the gate he leaned over and, unbuttoning my shirt pocket, slipped something into it. We shook hands and he left. When I examined my pocket I found a tightly folded ten-dollar bill. Then I really did cry.

Eventually, of course, the two years passed and I got back to town. I got a permanent assignment to *Fortune* and settled down to learn the business of magazine production. I made many friends at the office, moving from one apartment and one roommate to another. I began to meet space-buyers and people in the agencies, copy-writers and photographers, people like that. I made good money and saw a lot of new things but I didn't meet anybody like Bella and Angelo. I heard from them once in a while and I tried to do things for them when I could. I bought Bella a portable TV one Christmas, I remember. It helped a lot because she was still unable to get out at all. And once I witnessed Angelo's will. It was pretty simple: 'I leave everything I have to my beloved sister, Bella Mazzaferro, because she has taken care of our mother.'

This floored me completely. It was the first time I had ever realized that they were brother and sister, not husband and wife. I knew they didn't use the same bedroom but I'd always thought it was because of Bella's leg, or maybe because she wanted to sleep near Mama, to keep an eye on her. The thing was, they looked alike the way a husband and wife often get to look alike and they were closer to each other than any other two people I knew.

I didn't see an awful lot of them for quite a while. Just after I got back from the army I heard that Mama had had some kind of a stroke. I didn't find out how bad it was until I witnessed the will nearly two years later. She was completely paralysed and totally blind. At very rare moments she could speak, and all she ever said then was nasty criticism of the way Bella took care of her. Bella was literally a slave to her, cared for her all the time, kept her clean, gave her hypodermics, made her bed, fed her. This went on for several years, about five years, until, a month ago, Mama died.

I went down to see them as soon as I heard. The apartment was different, quieter, and they seemed like a pair of lost little mice who didn't know what to do with themselves. They couldn't seem to understand that Mama had died. Bella sat in the kitchen looking out the window with a blank look on her face as though she couldn't find anybody to do things for. Angelo told me about the funeral.

'The relatives buried her,' he said, twisting his hands together. 'Out in Queens, the only cemetery with room, they're all crowded. I never thought she'd die. I should have made arrangements.'

'Weren't you at the funeral, either of you?'

'No. But we paid for it, the plot, flowers, and a stone.'

'How come you couldn't make it?'

'I had a day-shift. I had to have the money. And without me Bella couldn't get out of the house. They took care of everything and we paid for it.'

'Well, look,' I said, 'now that Bella has so much time on her hands, shouldn't she get out from time to time?'

'I guess she should,' he said. 'I'll see about it.'

'Let me know if I can help.'

'I will,' he said eagerly. 'I will.'

A week or two later he called me at the office, wondering if I could borrow a car and take them for a drive.

'Bella thinks we should visit the cemetery and leave some flowers. She feels funny about Mama.'

'Is she very upset?'

'She just feels funny. I think the two of us can get her up and down the stairs. It might take a little time.'

'I'll make time,' I said.

I don't believe you need a car, living in Manhattan, and I don't have one, so last weekend I borrowed a car from Ed Mahoney, a jerk in the promotion department, and Sunday afternoon I drove around to 24th Street. We had the damnedest time getting Bella down the stairs but she enjoyed every minute of it. She was a lot heavier than you might figure too. Once she fell on top of Angelo and nearly squashed him flat and once she let her brace down on my toes. Laughing all the time! You'd have thought it was an excursion up the Hudson. When we finally got away, I drove across the island and out the Midtown Tunnel to Queens.

Manhattan is bad enough but Queens on Sunday afternoon is jammed with traffic all going out this parkway or that for a look at the country, if you can call it that. More like a look at the sub-divisions. Driving in heavy traffic always bothers me and after about half an hour of it I began to feel depressed; you know that pain you get across your shoulders? Everybody was in such a hell of a rush. We were on that parkway that goes out past Idlewild, busy as hell, and it was starting to rain.

I don't know. The whole trip was depressing.

We got there around two-thirty; it's a great big Catholic cemetery right next to the parkway, a huge place which probably got started in the thirties when Long Island real estate opened up. Some of the monuments looked as though they might be fairly old, perhaps twenty years, but to tell the truth, the place looked like one more great big sub-division. Not peaceful, I mean.

We drove around inside for quite a while, trying to get our bearings. Angelo and Bella had no idea where Mama was supposed to be. They didn't act very disturbed about it, just kept chattering away in Italian, much too fast for me to follow. I had to watch the roads anyway; they wound all over the place and it was raining harder than before. I asked Angelo if he knew where to look.

'Distant View,' he said. 'That's where she is.'

'What's that, part of the cemetery?'

'Yeah. The low-priced quality part.'

The next gardener I saw, I put my head out of the window, getting soaking wet.

'Hey!' I said. 'Where's the Distant View sub-division?'

'You're in the wrong place, buddy. This is a cemetery.'

'You know what I mean. Don't be funny.'

'Did you say "Distant View"?'

'Yeah.'

'Northeast section of the property. Poverty Row.'

'What did you say?'

'Northeast corner; it's brand new, just developed. You can't miss it. Right beside the highway.'

'Thanks, comic,' I said.

It wasn't too hard to find after that; you had to keep left and follow along beside the parkway. Soon we saw a sign with the name 'Distant View' in big letters. I stopped the car. Honest to God, I never saw a meaner-looking landscape in my life.

It looked like a giant's mudpie. The whole section was perhaps three acres between the cemetery road and the highway, on a steep slope. No trees, not a goddamn shrub. You could see that the hillside had originally been flat and hollow. Some landscape gardener had decided that it should have a convex roll down to the highway. So they had simply bulldozed a few tons of sticky clay on to the side of the hill and sodded it with the rankest kind of cheap grass. You could see the fresh mud in gullies criss-crossing the hillside and all around the edges; the grass needed trimming badly and the rain wasn't improving the scene.

Down the hill a hundred yards in front of us the cars were whizzing past on the parkway. It was no place for restful slumber. The queerest thing was that there weren't any monuments or markers. No flowers either. Just this expanse of muddy hillside and coarse grass. I began to wonder how we'd ever find Mama.

When we got out of the car I told Bella that she ought to stay inside for a few minutes but she paid no attention. She acted very excited and didn't seem to mind the rain. We moved awkwardly down the hill; the lumps of mud under the sod made the footing tricky and I was afraid Bella might fall heavily. She kept her feet surprisingly well considering the parcel she had in her arms, a great big bundle of newspapers. All the time I kept looking for markers or grave plates but I couldn't see a thing. I wanted to get Angelo by himself so when the ground smoothed out a bit I moved forward and he followed me.

'Jesus, Angelo,' I said. 'I don't know how we're going to find her. Didn't you get a marker or anything?'

'I can't understand it,' he said. 'I paid for one.'

'Who did you give the money to?'

'My brother Joe. He said he'd take care of it.'

'I guess he did, all right. How much did you give him?'

'Five hundred sixty-five dollars. All we had saved.'

'It's my guess that Joe got away with about three hundred bucks. There's nothing to mark the place and there sure as hell aren't any flowers.'

'What'll we do?'

'You stay here. I'll go and find somebody who knows the layout.'

They didn't want to go back to the car. As I climbed back up the hill I looked over my shoulder and saw them moving aimlessly around in circles on the hillside. I crossed the crest of the hill and ran down the road, hoping I'd see the administration building somewhere. I was getting mad.

After stumbling around on those winding roads for a quarter of an hour I found it, a big stone building with a display window full of sample monuments with sample inscriptions to John and Mary Doe. I hurried inside and spoke to the receptionist.

'Where can I find the manager?'

'Is there anything I can do?'

'You can direct me to whoever is in charge around here,' I said. 'That's what you can do.'

'Is there something wrong, sir?'

'You're damn right there is.' I was rude to her but I couldn't help it. The whole thing was so fouled up. 'I want to see the plans of the cemetery.'

'I'm sorry, sir,' she said. 'We do not provide that information for the general public.'

'You're going to provide it for me,' I said, raising my voice. I was taught never to raise my voice. 'I want to find where somebody's buried. Are you trying to tell me you haven't got that information?'

'Oh, yes. We have it in the files.'

'Well, get it.'

She got up and went into an office at the back of the room. In a minute a fat little man came out, followed by the girl.

'This is Mr. Lascelles, the superintendent,' she said. 'He'll be happy to take care of you.'

'How do you do, sir,' he said. I didn't much care for his manner.

'Listen,' I said, 'how do I find out where somebody's planted in this pasture of yours?'

'A relative?'

'The mother of some close friends.'

'Not an immediate relative?'

'Not of mine. Her son and daughter are out there in the rain, looking for the old lady. I want to know where she is.'

'The grave is unmarked?'

'What do you think I'm doing here?'

'I don't know sir, I'm sure,' he said. 'If you could make yourself clear ... Would the grave be in one of our newer projects?'

'Distant View, I think it is. Mrs. Mazzaferro.'

'Ah, Distant View. One of our low-cost areas. Our minimal service. The cemetery, sir, is not responsible for marking such projects, although we sometimes do so for reference purposes.'

He drummed his fingers on the counter, looking worried.

'Distant View is a relatively new project. There haven't been more than twenty interments in the area. In a few years, when it fills up, we may insert plot-line-markers which form an accurate grid. But just at present the plans are our chief guide to the area.'

'You *do* have plans?'

'Oh, yes. They aren't as accurate as the markers. You must remember that the marking and care of the grave are an optional additional service which the mourners have not cared to provide in this case.'

'The real mourners weren't at the funeral.'

'Yes, I understand,' he said, dolefully. 'In such cases the more distant connections often fail to take advantage of our optional services.'

'Tell me,' I said, 'what would be the bare minimum charge for a funeral, the casket, the grave, and all the rest of it?'

'Depending on your choice of mortician, and including service in our Distant View project, the total fee should run around two hundred and twenty five dollars and change.'

'I can see what's happened,' I said. 'Get the plans and let's get started.'

'Really, sir,' he said. 'I can't come with you. I've got a lot of business to attend to.'

'I don't know how to read your damn plans,' I said. 'Now either get your coat on, or I'll make trouble for you. I've got press and radio connections in the city, good connections. If you don't come across I'll see that you get a lot of unwelcome publicity. These people are out here in the rain wandering around looking for their mother, don't you understand?' He fumbled and grumbled for a minute but in the end he came, bringing the plans with him. He didn't say much; the rain bothered him too.

When we got there, Bella and Angelo were still circling around, getting nowhere. They looked pretty forlorn.

'This is Mr. Lascelles, the superintendent. He's going to help us find the place.'

'Thanks very much,' Angelo said. Lascelles paid no attention to him but turned to me instead.

'Standard plots in this section are ten feet by eight, providing a margin of two feet around every grave.'

'Roomy,' I said.

'Oh, yes,' he said. 'A very commodious arrangement.'

'How do we find the individual grave?'

'Look at the plan,' he said, unrolling it. 'The graves are numbered from east to west and lettered from south to north, from the top of the hill to the parkway.'

'Go on.'

'Mrs. Mazzaferro is Number 22-F. You'll have to pace, let's see, twenty-two times eight, that's, uh, a hundred seventy-six feet. Better say fifty-nine paces of a yard each.'

'Uh-huh.'

'The letter F indicates the sixth division down from the top of the hill. Six times ten – sixty feet. Twenty paces.'

'Very systematic,' I said. 'Just like the Stadium.'

'It does the job,' he said. 'Do you want me to stay here while you pace it off?'

'That might be a good idea,' I said. 'Angelo can help me.'

We walked down to the end of the section, as far to the east as we could get; Lascelles kept motioning us further back. Finally he shouted: 'OK. Stop! Take fifty-nine paces in this direction.'

I told Angelo to go and stand in the middle of the field to keep me on a straight line. We got lined up and I paced off the distance, trying to keep each step as close to a yard as I could. When I had taken fifty-nine I stopped and spoke to Angelo.

'Stand here and I'll measure down from the top.' I climbed back up and Lascelles came over. 'Do you need me any more?' he asked. 'I'm wet through.'

'I guess not. Thanks for your help.'

'You won't put this in the papers or anything?'

'No. But you ought to have some markers.'

'Later on we will.' Then he left. He really was soaked.

I got in line with Angelo and paced off the twenty yards down from the hilltop; then he and Bella joined me and we took a careful look around. We could see no depression in the ground where a new grave might have settled; the grass, matted and thick above the ground, made that impossible. Bearing in mind the rough and ready measurements we'd made, we couldn't have been perfectly accurate anyway.

'It's a hit-and-miss business,' I told them. 'She's somewhere around in here.'

'Where?' said Bella.

I made a circling motion with my arm, pointing at the ground. 'Her head should be within ten square feet of here.'

They followed my finger with their eyes. Then, quite arbitrarily, Bella selected a large knotted clump of grass and mud. 'There!' she said.

'That's as close as we can get.'

They stood there looking silently at this lump of grass and mud for a minute or two. Then Bella unwrapped her parcel and let the wind carry the newspapers away down towards the parkway. It wasn't flowers but some kind of plant, with long spiky green leaves, in a flower-pot. She bent over and set the pot on the ground. Then, with a twisting motion, she screwed the bottom of the pot solidly into the mud, about four inches deep. Then, by God, the two of them knelt down, on that soaking sod, in a heavy rain, and recited the Rosary. It took about ten minutes. I could feel rainwater running down my back inside my shirt. Finally they got up. I was just going to ask them if they were ready to go when a funny thing happened. The two of them were staring at each other, looking different than usual – I wouldn't have recognized them. A great big smile came across Bella's face. Angelo started to laugh softly.

'Mama's really gone now,' Bella said.

Angelo echoed her. 'Really gone. For good.'

Without a word to me they turned away and helped each other up the hillside to the car.

Nobody spoke a word all the way home in the car. I kept thinking it over; I felt as though they'd been laughing at me. Either I'd cheated them, or they'd cheated me, or somebody pulled a fast one somewhere. The whole thing was very mixed up.

A Faithful Lover

'DEAR FRIENDS IN CHRIST,' began the celebrant, 'we are directed by our beloved shepherd the Cardinal to instruct the faithful on seven occasions during the liturgical year concerning the sacraments. For seven Sundays annually, in obedience to this wise pastoral direction, we put before you the dogmas of the Church and their generally accepted theological consequences concerning these sources of spiritual life.'

He cleared his throat and stole a glance at his watch.

'My subject this Sunday is baptism, the sacrament of innocence. As you know, dear Catholic people, a sacrament is the outward and visible sign of an interior activity of grace, moving in the human soul by the love of God. When he instituted the sacraments during his public life, Our Blessed Lord so ordained, that with the administration of the outward sign, the appropriate grace should always be donated by God, who is of course in no sense the prisoner of the sacraments. But the sacramental sign is somehow, in a certain sense, a true secondary cause of grace in the human soul. And each sacrament has its own efficacy and its special external form.

'The external form of baptism is an infusion of holy water upon the head of the candidate, accompanied by certain prayers, in the presence of certain witnesses. It is usually administered to infants and is peculiarly the sacrament of children and the perfectly innocent.

'And what does this external sign suggest? Baptism is a cleansing of invisible defects in the most inward recesses of our nature. For each of us, my friends, is born into this life not indeed totally corrupt, but wounded in our nature – we are the heirs of our first parents and the magnitude of their offence was such as to destroy forever the entire race, were it not for the Incarnation, Redemption and Atonement of Christ, the Second Person of the Blessed Trinity, who Himself instituted and magnanimously received this sacrament, although His Human Nature needed no such cleansing.

'Baptism is the first of the sacraments. It may not possess the centrality, the splendour and unutterable mystery of the Eucharist, but it is logically prior to all the other sacraments for without it our fully human lives cannot begin. It is fitting therefore that our children receive this grace at the earliest possible moment.'

Here the priest paused, poured himself a glass of water and drank thirstily. As he drank the congregation moved to and fro in their seats and a quiet sigh spread around the church.

In his wooden pew John Carroll shifted restlessly with the rest of the parishioners, scarcely aware of the tiny easing motion because the sermon, though its doctrines were familiar to him from infancy, had captured his whole attention. The priest's brief pause allowed him a moment's inattention and he glanced sharply sidewise at Maria, sitting obediently like a schoolchild beside him.

Of what haven't we been guilty, he thought suddenly, what horrors have we left undone? He stole another sly glance at Maria, thinking thankfully of her approaching regeneration. He thought his own life a continual war against the consequences of Original Sin. Soon Maria would be liberated entirely, given a fresh start. Often, how often, had he tried to merit a plenary indulgence so that he might start over: but his fulfilment of the annexed conditions was always open to question.

She felt him watching her and turning gave him a quick and loving regard. She has, he vowed, the attitudes of devotion, if not the full reality which must come after. Until now, without the strong sacramental graces, what could her life have been? He wondered how it was that uninstructed and for practical purposes an utter pagan she had nonetheless kept unimpaired her air of virginity and innocence. You'd think it would show in her face and walk, he thought savagely, she can't have lived any better than a naturally good life. I wish I knew more about her. He wondered about the effects of living without sanctifying grace, could one possibly avoid the death of mortal sin? Were Aristotle and Virgil unregenerate and damned ... where had Dante pigeonholed them? Not all atheists were necessarily inevitably depraved. Why? How could they manage without grace?

He despaired of reaching a conclusion and renewed his attention to the sermon.

'As the babe is thus given the power to live a Christian life, so is the convert, the adult who embraces our Holy Faith. Such a man or woman, newly baptized, resembles the pure infant, without stain of sin. Should such a person die immediately after receiving the sacrament, his soul would fly directly to the arms of God for there could be in him not the smallest guilt. Strive then, my friends, to lead your non-Catholic friends to the Faith that they may be purified from sin and guilt. Pray that all men may receive the healing water of the holy sacrament of baptism. In the Name of the Father and of the Son and of the Holy Ghost.' Descending from the pulpit the priest crossed to the altar and began the Credo. John followed him with his eyes and a part of his mind but his most inward thoughts were elsewhere.

Afterwards Maria and John struggled through the retreating congregation to the winter sunshine outside. They strolled through the grounds of the college next to the church and made their way up Queen's Park Crescent. John had received Holy Communion so, as they were accustomed to do, they went to a nearby restaurant and enjoyed a leisurely breakfast; it was their favourite time of the week, when they felt closest to one another.

'I'M GLAD you heard that sermon,' said John, 'does it help to make things clearer?'

'I understand more and more as time passes,' she said.

'Nothing troubles you? You can accept it all?'

'Oh, yes, yes, yes, with thanks. You don't know how things were in Germany after the war. No one cared, no one helped us with religious things, we were so beaten and there seemed to be nothing left.'

'It is a shame about your parents.'

'I know they weren't believers,' she said hesitantly, 'and they had the same sort of education as mine, after the first war. It was even worse for them.' She paused, smiling at him. 'But my father was an honest scholar, though he wasn't a Christian.'

'And your mother ...'

'... followed my father in everything, she wanted no life of her own, never felt the lack of it.'

'You are going to have your own life, Maria. I guarantee it.'

'I hope so,' she said, laughing softly.

'Do you know, the sermon made me think about you very hard. Will you feel different when you've been received?'

'I don't think so,' she said, blushing, 'I've not been a great and terrible sinner.'

'You will be made utterly perfectly innocent. We must try to preserve that.'

'John, darling,' she said, 'one remains human, after all.'

'Hypothetically you could remain innocent and pure indefinitely.'

'I have always been pure.'

'Naturally pure.'

'Is that not sufficient? I've done no harm to anyone.'

'There is a distinction,' he said, feeling his thoughts begin to whirl and run. 'It is a hard line to draw. But you will feel the difference, once you've been baptized. You will feel God within you.'

'It will not be so hard to be truthful and good?'

He sighed. 'It's always hard.'

'But you will always be there to help me.'

'Yes, of course.'

And they went on smiling and gazing happily at each other, finishing their breakfast. When they rose to go, John seized Maria's arm manfully, and tucked it under his own. He felt with intense pleasure the motion, the pulse of her warm animation, in the soft limb.

FOR FOUR generations there had been a tradition amongst the Carrolls that at least one of them in every descending generation should have a vocation to the religious life. None of John's six older brothers and sisters had received such a call and he, the youngest, had been expected, almost as a matter of course, to consider the priesthood as his natural profession. However in his last years in high school he had begun to develop a great interest in mathematics and physics; he had been fortunate in his teachers and began to wonder if he had found out his real call in life. His family had been troubled by the idea and entreated him to try life in the seminary for a least a year or two.

'After all,' said his mother, 'you could still study mathematics. You might teach in a college, many priests do.'

At the seminary he took readily to the more abstract aspects of his studies in theology and the philosophy of Scholasticism, but it became more and more clear that his mind and his whole person, his character, was not that of a pastor or a moral theologian, but instead that of some breed of speculative analyst, a physicist perhaps, a logician or metaphysician. He was an intense believer but he quite certainly had no religious vocation. His superiors advised him, kindly but in the strongest terms, not to attempt to proceed to the subdiaconate. After many disturbing interviews with his parents, he left the seminary.

He enrolled in honour science at the university, taking many minor courses in the department of philosophy. Here the indifference of the scientists to questions of metaphysics, and the heterodox and ordinarily agnostic professions of the philosophers, unsettled him more and more. In his third year at the university he began to feel the symptoms of marked instability, which he was the first to recognize. He very sensibly took medical and even psychiatric advice and was at last told that his intense engagement with his studies might bring on a serious breakdown. On the advice of his doctors, he gave up the university, at least for a while.

His family had regarded him as its most brilliant member. It was such a cruel blow, they all insisted, to see his talent going to waste. They could see nothing wrong with him; he seemed perfectly composed. At last he found a small room in a downtown boarding house where he could be quiet. When he found a job as demonstrator in a physics lab, he thought he might be happy. He moved all his books into his room and spent his spare time in solitary reading, chiefly the works of the mystics and the great metaphysicians. Lately he had been reading the voluntarists, Eckhart and Tauler, later writers like Boehme, Swedenborg, Law, sometimes Blake and Schelling, and most recently the theosophists. Somewhat in theosophical style, he had started to write down his own religious reflections.

Tonight he sat writing at his desk, the boarding house was

still. 'With what clear evidence,' he wrote, 'with what splendid truth do we consider baptism the most excellent of the mercies of God. For consider the soul in its unregenerate state, raging as a wolf for the pleasures of its bodily housing, sinking into the belly and the genitals, seeing not by the clear light of Heavenly illumination but by the black light of the senses. The still centre of the universe glows with a wordless music but the soul is whirled to the farthest edges of being, where cold winds whistle all night and an interior fire consumes.' He paused and licked the end of his pencil, lost in thought. Then he resumed.

'And now relieved by an infusion of water the soul leaps up like a hart in the chase, moving free at a single leap from the shackles of this earthly state, able and ready in a moment to rejoin the source of all things, to reascend the course of pure water. How noble a libation and how meet a sacrifice! The lamblike innocent thirsts for the source; it pants and struggles towards the well-head. What an excellent offering to the Lord, what a perfect gift, unspotted lamb, innocent spirit.'

He turned off his lamp, bent his head over his desk, and tried to meditate calmly. In the stillness he felt himself to be at the living centre of things, he felt the rise and warmth of his excitement, the world swirling around him vortically. He raised his eyes in the dark, seeing with utter clarity.

He continued this regimen of severe meditation until the night, many weeks later, when Maria was to be received into the Church; by then he felt himself ready for the trial. He wondered what he should do with a wife, not being himself a person given to easy unions. But he had discovered Maria all alone, a stranger unable to speak the language, struggling with her studies, nearly despairing, and he had raised her to this. What would she be to him now?

His mother was to be the necessary witness at the ceremony, so she and his father came to the church. Maria and a girl acquaintance were already there. Promptly at seven-thirty, Father Neumann, who had instructed Maria, came out of the sacristy and beckoned the small party towards the rail of the baptistry. He talked in a whisper to Maria, showing her what she must do.

'You are to state formally that you have never been baptized before,' he said, 'and you must make a formal profession of faith in the chief dogmas of the Church. You can read your profession from this.' He handed her a printed sheet of paper. Then priest and initiate went to the centre of the baptistry, where she knelt to make her profession and to pray. John and the others seated themselves in a pew near the baptismal font.

'She has a lot of courage,' muttered John's father. 'It's a lonely thing to do.'

John nodded wordlessly, his eyes fixed on Maria. He heard her whispering of mysteries and then reciting the Creed.

'I believe in the Holy Ghost, the Holy Catholic Church, the Communion of Saints, the forgiveness of sins, the resurrection of the body, and life everlasting.'

Father Neumann accompanied her to the baptismal font and John's mother came forward to take her place as witness; the actual baptism followed, a touching and impressive ritual. In a few moments it was over and a second priest moved out of the shadows and indicated a confessional. Maria followed him and the others retired to an adjoining parish office to wait for her.

'I remember,' said John's father jovially, 'when our banns were published. It was in this very church over thirty years ago.'

'Father Fessenden was pastor then,' said Father Neumann politely.

'That's right,' said Mr. Carroll. 'What a time I had with him. First I couldn't persuade him to put our banns up. There was no impediment, you understand, he just didn't remember. He was beginning to fail.'

'I was one of his curates when he died.'

'Were you now, Father? Well, do you know, when I finally got the banns started, I couldn't get them stopped, they went on and on for six weeks. I had to go to Father Fessenden and beg him: "Look, Father, if you please, no more banns. That's enough."'

Everyone laughed heartily at this. Father Neumann turned to John, smiling, and said, 'That's a wonderful girl you have there, John. I never knew a convert to see the magnificence of the Church the way she does.'

'She is enormously sensitive,' said John coolly, 'she understands things instinctively.'

'She's too good to live,' said his mother, fondly.

'On the contrary,' said John, 'she's not good enough, like the rest of us.'

His remark chilled the tone of the conversation for a moment and then the silence was dissipated by Maria's sudden reappearance. They all began to gabble cheerfully, to ask her how she felt, to make little jokes about the terrors of the confessional.

'He didn't keep you long,' said Mr. Carroll.

'No. It was easy.'

'I'll bet he gave you a good stiff penance, at least two decades of the Rosary.' This was an old family joke.

'No,' she said innocently, 'an Our Father and a Hail Mary.'

'You must have been behaving yourself lately.'

She blushed and turned to thank Father Neumann. The party rose to go, looking for overcoats and talking about streetcars. John took Maria by the arm and they turned to the door.

'We'll be seeing you soon, John?' asked Father Neumann.

'Oh, very soon.'

In a flurry of handshakes the group dispersed. Mr. and Mrs. Carroll walked towards the street to catch an uptown streetcar. Maria's girl-friend scuttled away to a late movie. John led Maria through the darkened college grounds towards Queen's Park.

'We'll go for a little walk,' he said kindly.

He led her along one of the gravel paths towards the centre of the park, near the bandstand. In the early summer twilight this path was a favourite of young engaged couples. Now, in February, it was abandoned. The icy stillness of the place, the hard gravel which rang under their steps, the silence, oppressed Maria more and more as they came to the centre. She had been in a mood of feverish excitement during the ceremony but it was wearing off, leaving a spent flatness behind. She shuddered at the cold and was surprised to feel an answering shudder, more violent than her own, in John's arm.

At last they reached the centre of the park and drew in under the great shadow of the bandstand. In front of them stood a large stone drinking fountain with four spouts. In the summer, children played around the fountain, spraying each other with mouthfuls of cool water. But tonight the fountain was boarded over for the winter. For a moment they stared at the big lump of

stone, sharing something inexpressible. Then he turned to her.
'I must do this,' he said unsteadily.

'What is it, darling?' she asked, her thoughts numbed by the
February chill. But he turned away, showing her his back. He
unbuttoned his overcoat and drew out a foot-long stainless-
steel knife. He looked over his shoulder, fixing his aim, and then
holding the handle of the knife in both hands he swung around,
lunging heavily forward, and his aim was accurate. The blade
sank deeply into the girl's neck, instantly depriving her of the
power of speech; her eyes flew open, bright with terror.

As she fell, blood flowed from the gash like a fountain. She
was lying on her side, moving slightly. He wrenched the blade
free and swung again, this time nearly severing the head. There
had been no sound.

Covering his eyes he turned away and walked around the side
of the bandstand to the stairs which led to the upper platform.
There he sank down, dropping the knife, and put his aching
head in his arms, and let himself begin to shudder. He could see
her feet around the arc of the bandstand. He rested, letting the
shudders spend themselves, and soon he grew calmer.

A little while later he saw a figure on a bicycle coming from
the west side of the park. He rose and unhurriedly began to
move back in the direction of the church. In spite of himself he
felt a powerful impulse to conceal himself in the bare clumps of
shrubbery dotting the frozen park but at this time of year they
would provide no cover. Instead he held on, walking decisively
up the hard path. Far behind he heard a voice and then a
muffled shout; then he heard several voices and more shouting.
When he reached the edge of the park he was almost running.
Swiftly he crossed the crescent and entered the college grounds,
passing silently through archways towards the rectory. He
knocked on the door and soon the housekeeper appeared.

'Oh, it's you, Mr. Carroll,' she said, 'did you forget something?'

'I must see Father Neumann for a moment.'

'Is it urgent? I believe he's gone upstairs. He isn't well, you
know.'

'Would you please enquire, Mrs. Daley? Ask him to see me.'

'All right, sir. Just sit down in the parlour.'

He sat there for fifteen minutes, smoking idly and estimating the likelihood of his having been followed. At times he had a dreadful suspicion that there were crowds outside the rectory; each time he realized that it was an illusion and he was amazed at the power of these hallucinations. At length the priest appeared in the doorway.

'What is it, John?' he asked. 'It's growing late.'

'Maria is dead, Father. I killed her. She's lying over in the park.'

'Is she alone?'

'She's been found. I heard them shouting as I came away.'

Father Neumann looked away from John, rolling his pipe between his hands and then, with a start, putting it in his mouth. There was a pause while he filled the pipe, lit it, and began to draw upon it. He began to stare at John unblinkingly, his face impassive.

'You don't ask why I did it.'

'You believe too much, John, more than you need to believe.'

'She's in Heaven. She went directly to the arms of God.'

'No one will think of that. You're going to suffer terribly for this, you'll be treated like a murdering lunatic. You'll be in an asylum for the rest of your life, and that will be an unending horror. Did you think of that?'

'I thought of everything.'

'You forgot those who loved her.'

'No one knew her. No one loved her but me.'

Father Neumann clenched his fists convulsively. 'I loved her. She grasped the Faith better than anyone I ever taught, and she loved it.'

'Well, she's dead now,' he said brutally. 'What do you propose to do about it?'

'There's nothing for me to do, John. You'll have to do everything.'

'I tell you, I did it for love.'

'Oh, you're not a murderer, you're a superstitious fool. I don't know for whose love you did it, but you've taken the power of God into your own hands. No one dares do that.'

'I'd better let them know where to come.'

'Yes, there's a telephone in the office.'

When the police came, they swarmed in the parish grounds, over the cold flower beds, carrying searchlights and canisters of tear-gas, which they didn't need. They filled the rectory with bewildering voices, with cross-questionings and avowals. Finally they led the prisoner towards the door and only there did John make any show of resistance. He turned in the doorway, looking at Father Neumann who stood at the top of the stairs, and then at the police officers on either side of him. His face dissolved.

He cried: 'You don't understand, any of you. You don't know, you don't know.' He howled: 'See what I spared her!'

The Strategies of Hysteria

MY LANDLADY, Mrs. J. Delta Williams, is a hard, tough, cus-tomer. She has a marvellously preserved ancient Cadillac, the only one-storey house in West Hartford (she put it up just before the zoning restriction went into effect) and every major appliance. She also has a foster-son, Eddie Coleman, whom she acquired from the State Welfare Board; they pay for his upkeep and she loses nothing on the deal.

Although she was the cherished spouse of the late Delta Wil-liams for over forty years, she never presented him with a child. I mean that just the way it sounds; she's a very odd duck. She belongs to all these offbeat religious groups like the Unity Church of Sedalia and the local Sect of Jesus! I've been shown some of her correspondence with the Unity and, believe me, it's pretty rarefied. I remember one morning at breakfast when she began to tell me all about her readings in philosophy.

'I'm like you,' she said. 'I like my reading deep.'

'I'm not so deep,' I said, politely.

'I've read all the philosophers,' she told me. 'Mrs. Eddy and that other one, that Swedish one.'

'Swedenborg?'

'Yes. And I read the life of that Greek thinker Aristocracies. That was most interesting.'

'Aristocracies?'

One day she had the local bookstore on the line, giving them a hard time. 'I want a copy of "Prose Works",' she kept saying. I could hear the clerk on the other end going mad.

'Prose Works. *Prose Works!* You must have it; it's a famous book. "Prose Works" by Mary Baker Eddy. What are you laughing at?' I'll never forget the night she began to tell me about reincarnation, the astral planes, and the life after death of cats and certain other household pets. No. No! No, on second thought let's not get involved with that – too complicated.

Before she got hold of Eddie Coleman she had another foster-child, a girl named Laura. When I first came to stay there, Laura used to telephone Mrs. Williams each morning to relate the latest catastrophes, apparently the girl was just naturally trouble-prone. When she'd been in high school she'd formed some kind of crazy liaison with one of the teachers who eventually got fired. Later on she married and had a couple of children and then the marriage went bust. From what Mrs. Williams says, I gather that Laura wasn't merely sinned against. Then she got married again and sure enough matters began to deteriorate. The landlord began to watch her through the windows at night so that she and her husband had to move. Then they had a hell of a time finding another place to live. Then they bought a houseful of furniture on time and lost it all. I've met Laura once or twice and she really is a very comely creature – probably didn't have much chance.

'She was always a trouble to me,' Mrs. Williams declared after one of these long recitals of woe. 'She's far too pretty for her own good.'

'She's extremely pretty,' I said, cautiously.

'Of course you realize,' she went on, 'I never could do anything with her. I didn't get her till she was eleven years old.'

'I see.'

'Yes. She was set in her ways. She was all *formed* then.'

'Oh?'

'Mind you, it's different with Eddie. He was only four when he came. Goodness, you should have seen him, such a puny scrawny specimen. He was so weak with rickets he could hardly walk. He was a mess.'

You ought to understand that Eddie was in the room while this conversation was proceeding. I avoided his eye.

'Mmmmhmmm,' she wound up. 'Eddie's father was certainly no good at all. And his mother was even worse. Smoked and drank.'

'I smoke and drink,' I said, out of pure loyalty to the group.

'Not like you,' she said, judiciously. 'They were immoderate all the time.'

'I'm immoderate about twice a week,' I told her. 'That's all I can afford.'

'You're never any trouble,' she said. 'It was different with Eddie's folks. The Welfare told me they were the talk of Bristol.'

'Eddie's not like that.'

'No,' she admitted, looking at him hard. 'But then he wasn't *formed* when I got him.'

Eddie called Mrs. Williams 'Maw' and sometimes went by her surname but she never addressed him as 'Son' or anything like that. And since he began to grow into adolescence he's begun to notice the disparity so that the last six months have been a continual wrangle.

One night just before Thanksgiving I came home and stood on the porch to smoke a cigarette before going in – Mrs. Williams doesn't allow smoking in her house. She claims it's because of an allergy but it resembles that attitude that thinks no pleasure moral but one's own. Anyway, I was standing on the porch when Eddie came out and stood beside me silently. I try to encourage him to talk about himself and finally he muttered: 'Thanksgiving weekend!'

'Yeah. It's coming right along.'

'Will you be going home?'

'I think so,' I said. 'I've got five days off.'

'Do you have Thanksgiving dinner in Canada?'

'Not this weekend. We have Thanksgiving early in October. Why?'

'I just wondered.'

He fell silent again for a moment and sidled up and down the porch fidgeting. I finished my cigarette and lit another. I had plenty of work to do but I hated to run out on him. He was always very quick to notice when I didn't feel like talking. From time to time he'd come into my room and tell me about his school work. Eventually Mrs. Williams stopped him because she felt he was being a nuisance. He wasn't, really.

'Going to be clear and warm tomorrow,' I said, looking at the sky.

'If the wind moves around it may rain,' he said. 'The paper says rain.' He was getting to be the worst little pessimist you ever saw, contradicting every reasonable hope. He reminded me of a much smaller child who'll pluck at his mother's skirts, get under her feet, generally annoy her – what they call 'asking for a spanking.' Where the child is really eager to be spanked just to be reassured that someone cares enough to punish him. That was the way Eddie used to disagree with me; he'd have been terribly pleased, I believe, if I'd growled at him but, being a guest in the house, I've never been able to decide how to tackle him. He certainly needed attention though and tonight something was bothering him. He finally came out with it. 'That Dr. Fenton!' he said with disgust.

Fenton is a retired dentist, an old pal of J. Delta Williams, who often visits the relict. They both belong to the 'Over 60 Club' and they go about together.

'What about the doctor?'

'He's taking my mother down the Parkway to dinner.'

'Tonight?'

'No. Thanksgiving. They're going with three other couples.'

I could see what was coming. 'What about you?'

'I have to go to my lousy old grandmother's.'

Of course he didn't want to go and I could see his point. The woman was his mother's mother and no bargain, a short, square, squatty type with a face that had nothing in it but empty meanness. He'd been away from that family since he was two years old, except for rare awful visits. It must have seemed like going back to jail.

'You'll meet some of your relatives and get to know them. It won't be so bad.'

'I don't want to get to know them.' He looked straight at me. 'I wish you were going to be here. Maybe we could eat together.'

'I'm not much on holidays,' I said. What could I do?

He looked at me for a minute and then went inside while I finished my second cigarette. Then I went inside too. As I went through the living-room Eddie was playing the radio very loud, switching it from station to station. Soon, I heard Mrs. Williams hollering at him to cut it out.

During the Christmas holidays things were comparatively quiet, *chez* Williams, or so I heard when I came back after New Year's. The two of them had taken a little trip together up to Maine, almost to the border. They'd exchanged Christmas gifts. Eddie, who loved to draw, had made some religious drawings in coloured pencils for Mrs. Williams, each with a touching sentiment (they both thought) lettered underneath. Dr. Fenton was out of town for a while, in Florida, I believe.

But inevitably the bickering began again. One night last week I heard them going at it but I didn't pay too much attention until they began to get pretty personal. Then I listened. It wasn't eavesdropping. I've told them twenty times that I can hear everything that's said in the house and they either don't care or have no notion of decent privacy.

'You're going to do as I say,' Mrs. Williams kept saying.

Rebellious grunt from Eddie.

'Yes, you are, little Mister. Now put those silly crayons away and do your homework.'

No response.

'Eddie, are you going to do what I tell you?'

'I'm busy!'

'Busy wasting time! You'll never get anywhere with those drawings. They're just no good.'

'They're good.'

'Eddie, don't be silly. You get yourself a nice trade and forget about this nonsense. You told me you wanted to go into electronics.'

'I've changed my mind.'

'You're too young to have any opinion. Now I'm telling you. You're going to finish junior high. Then you're going to march downtown to trade school.'

'I am not. I'm going to go to art school.'

'With whose money?'

'I'll get scholarships. The teacher says I can.'

'That's silly,' she bawled. 'It might be different if Mr. Williams were alive but he isn't. I've got all I can do to keep you.'

'I'm going to do what I want,' he said weakly.

'You'll do as I tell you until you're twenty-one. Besides, you'll have to go into the army sooner or later. You haven't time to fool around with this.'

He apparently didn't answer because she went on louder than before. 'Look,' she said in a voice that was supposed to clinch the argument, 'look at me. I took a course up to the college in design. What did I ever get out of it? Tell me that!'

He said nothing.

'I've written poetry all my life,' she said. 'What did that ever get me?'

'I won't go to trade school.'

'What's the matter with trade school?'

'The kids say it's boring.'

'You're probably too stupid to get into trade school. Look at your marks!'

'I got those marks on purpose.'

'You're so smart. I suppose you failed on purpose.'

'I did,' he said defiantly. 'I'll never get into trade school.'

'I'll tell your grandmother and she'll fix you. I'll send you back to her and you can see what she says.'

'Oh, shut up!' he wailed.

It occurred to me that I might be able to break it up tactfully so I wandered through the living-room to the porch. They were silent as I passed but as I closed the front door I heard them break out again. When I went back inside Mrs. Williams paused in full cry and turned to me. 'Look at Mr. Twombley,' she said with a grin. 'He's got some sense. He's been to training school and now he's got a nice easy job up to the college, teaches a few hours a week and he can fool around with his writing in his time off. Isn't that right?' she appealed to me.

'The job's easy enough.'

'There,' she cut in triumphantly. 'Get yourself a trade and you can do your drawing as a hobby.' He looked sulky.

'If you really want to be an artist,' I told him rather pompously, 'you'll have to work much harder than you would at trade school.'

'What did I tell you?' said Mrs. Williams, although, strictly speaking, my argument didn't quite square with hers. 'To make money as an artist you have to be good. You'll never be any good.'

'I wasn't thinking of the money,' I put in.

'What else is it good for?' There wasn't any answer to that, of course; she had me.

'Well, anyhow,' I said bewilderedly, 'don't force Eddie to decide before he's old enough to know what he wants.'

'He's old enough to be sensible.' She turned on him again. 'I can change my mind too, you know. Two can play at that game.'

'What are you talking about?' he asked worriedly.

'You know what I'm talking about. When Mr. Williams died I promised you I'd never get married again. I'd just look after you. Well, I've changed my mind, that's all. I'll find a nice gentleman my age and get married again and you, Mister Artist, you'll be out in the cold.' His face flushed heavily and he didn't say anything.

'There,' she said. 'I guess we've heard the last of that.'

Before this last piece of brutality we both had to retreat. It was a mind beautifully, ruggedly, armed against understanding.

You have to realize that Eddie gets into a little trouble now and then. He'll throw a snowball and knock somebody's hat off, or cut across a lawn too often – every kid gets mixed up in this kind of thing. A night or two later, a policeman called at the house to explain that Eddie and one or two others had broken a window on the way home from school and that he was the only one who had been spotted. The woman who owned the house was screaming to the cops about the terrible loss she'd suffered, and about the general behaviour of today's teenagers, those notorious vandals. I suppose the cop thought to himself: 'Better throw a scare into the kid.'

He was talking to Mrs. Williams and Eddie when I came in, not taking the matter too seriously. I mean, it wasn't a question of Eddie's being dragged off to a cell, or appearing in juvenile court or anything, just a warning. He made some futile attempts to deny that he'd been mixed up in the affair. He was a transparent liar, couldn't come up with any convincing alibi, and finally had to admit that he'd done it.

'Listen, son,' the cop said, laughing, 'don't try to cover up. I'm not going to eat you alive but I know it was you.'

Mrs. Williams was hysterical for fear it might cost her something. 'You destructive little thing,' she kept squeaking. 'Breaking windows. Smashing milk-bottles. You stepped on the cat and broke her leg. The eggs fell off your bicycle. And now the police are after you. See?'

The policeman looked at me and half smiled.

'Was it a serious matter?' I asked him.

'Well, hardly life and death. But you'd have thought it was from the way Mrs. Whatsit down the street was hollering.'

'I'll bet!'

'Now look, Mrs. Williams,' he told her. 'We know your boy isn't a hoodlum. I'll just leave the lady your phone number and she can call you to arrange about paying for the window.' He edged towards the door.

'Was it one window or two?'

'One pane of glass in a cellar window, about eight inches by four. Don't pay for any more.' By now he was plainly feeling sorry for Eddie – kind of a neat peripeteia, I thought to myself. Detaching himself from Mrs. Williams with some difficulty, he got into the patrol car and drove hastily away.

The debate continued all through supper, see-sawing back and forth between Mrs. Williams and Eddie, with me as moderator. I felt like Dag Hammerskjold. By seven o'clock she'd managed to convict him of enough crimes, with the aid of some vivid inventions, that you'd have thought him the original Attila the Hun. Finally he just sat staring at his plate. At seven-thirty the phone rang – the injured lady down the street, determined to extract the last drop of self-justification and victory from the atrocity. I couldn't make out what she was saying because she spoke very fast. You could follow the general drift though because of Mrs. Williams' reactions which were pretty emphatically marked.

'_____ !' said the lady.

'Yes, this is Mrs. Williams. Yes.'

'_____ ,' faster and faster.

'He's been here ... About five o'clock.'

Eddie and I were listening to this dialogue with a kind of horrid fascination. The way Mrs. Williams was reacting to the whole business, you'd have thought he'd murdered somebody. The whole affair had been blown up out of all proportion and poor Eddie was the one who'd have to bear the disproportionate consequences. He was following her responses on the phone as though he'd been hypnotized. I didn't like seeing a boy his age under that much tension.

'_____ ,' squeaked the telephone.

'Not on your life,' said Mrs. Williams stoutly. 'The police told me exactly what was broken.'

'_____ .'

'Twenty-five dollars?' yelped Mrs. Williams. 'You're trying to cash in, are you? How many windows do you plan to fix?' It was becoming a low brawl.

'_____,' very assertive.

'I won't pay it,' said Mrs. Williams heroically.

'_____.'

'Very well. I'll tell you what to do. Submit your claim to the State Welfare Board. Yes, that's right. Send it to them; don't send it to me. Then, in about two years you'll get your money.' She began to laugh insultingly. 'That's right,' she said. 'I'm not responsible. He's no blood kin of mine.' Shaking all over with triumph and relief she hung up the phone.

I couldn't take my eyes off Eddie. He'd been living with her for ten years. Without his being aware of it, shame, disgust, horror, had been passing over his face. Now, as he looked at her, it was a crumpled face. I know, I thought to myself, I know. I know.

I think I better find myself a new place to live.

That 1950 Ford

I THINK THAT WEST HARTFORD is the finest place to live
in the whole world and the richest, and I should know. My husband – he was the late J. Delta Williams – and I opened up the
district thirty years ago and now there isn't a home in the better
part of town that cost less than twenty-five thousand dollars to
put up.

Delta was an independent realtor in a small way when we
decided to build and he was clever about houses even then. He
built me a forty-thousand-dollar house for a lot less than it
would have cost anybody else and then, of course, there were no
zoning restrictions in those days. In fact, Delta wrote the zoning restrictions. He put the money into our house where it
really meant something, not just for show. I still have the driest
cellar on the street and ours was the first and only one-storey
ranch-style house allowed in our zone.

You wouldn't believe what it looked like when we first came
– no sewers, no sidewalks, no trees, and *mud*, my goodness –
but now there are lots of trees. Everybody has a dog. We have
the best garbage collectors and police that money can buy, and
two wonderful shopping centres. It's true that the garbage collectors are pretty finicky; everything has to be drained and
filtered and sorted, tied in pink ribbon, you might say. And the
police ride around in new cars every year. But it's worth it for
the protection; they're up and down the street all night.

I wish Delta could see it, and perhaps he does, somewhere. I
know that his spirit – his 'genius' is what the Christian Science
folks call it – is here in West Hartford. He had so much to do
with the development and all the business part of building up
the town. But he passed beyond several years ago; it seems like
only yesterday but it was eight years. We were returning from
Florida when he had his stroke in a little place in South Carolina
and died in a motel. I wish he could have died in West Hartford
because we both loved it so much.

It was men like J. Delta Williams and Gus Frink who made
West Hartford what it was. Now that they've mostly gone, we

widows have to keep things the way they wanted them and it hasn't been easy. Builders have been trying to introduce the cheaper house; some places they've succeeded. The Jews have moved in. However we have only the nicest Jews, almost like real Nutmeggers. The others are all over on the north side of Albany Avenue, not really in West Hartford, proper, at all.

Lately there's been some Communist agitation to admit *Coloured!* But everyone in town, even the nicer Jews, closed ranks on the issue. It was inspiring.

I will say this for the nicer Jews, they keep up their property. But then, of course, they've got the money to do it. You take my next-door neighbours, the Lewisohns, for example. They aren't original with the street like I am but they were the first Jews who ever lived in West Hartford, that must be twenty years ago. They came from some place downtown and it must have been a big step up in the world for them and they've always taken care of their property. They repaint every year; they have a power mower and the lawn looks proper. They're just like anybody. Quiet and good neighbours who'll offer you a ride downtown. But they're quirky, too, quirky, I suppose everybody is some way or other. I have some little quirks too. Goodness, I'm entitled to them, a widow, after all. I've tried various religions. People laugh at me but since I had my vision I've been very interested in the whole question.

I don't tell about my vision to everyone. It's just that I had a vision of Delta in the afterlife. I won't go into it. I just mention it to show that I have some quirks of my own, so I can afford to be broadminded. After I had my vision I joined the Unity Church of Sedalia, Mo., and I've had more satisfaction from them than you could shake a stick at. Them and the Christian Science and the Rev. Mr. Oral Roberts, the healer.

I had my vision of my late beloved in the form of a ring of fire whirling around just below the ceiling in the parlour. He spoke to me, calling me by name.

'Don't let yourself moulder away, Alba,' he told me. He seemed to want me to have people around me, as I reasoned it out. I'd let myself become almost a recluse after he died. I thought about it for a while, and put a piece in the paper, and told them about it up to the college. I finally got myself a roomer, a nice young man. That's when the trouble began.

At first it was just that my young man started to watch the neighbours when he went out on the porch to smoke his cigarette. I don't allow smoking in my house. Others may like it and they can do as they please. But my roomer was very nice. I got him from the college. He would go outside and watch the neighbours, and especially Mr. Lewisohn washing his car.

Mr. Twombley – the roomer – was a polite young fellow, kind of shiftless. For some reason he didn't go to work at the college every day; he hung around the house a lot, claiming he was writing a book. He may have been but I never saw any traces of it. He spent most of his time talking to the neighbours or the postman or whoever came near the house. Most of all he talked to Mr. and Mrs. Lewisohn, being about the same age as their Norman, and being fascinated by the way Mr. Lewisohn cared for his car.

The Lewisohns had two cars, one for the Missus and one for the Mister. She had a big new Chrysler; oh, just a lovely car. 'A piece of merchandise' is what she called it. 'A lovely piece of merchandise.' I can hear her now.

Mr. Lewisohn's car was an old old pile of junk that he kept hanging on to for sentimental reasons, I suppose. It was kind of an embarrassment to the neighbourhood to see that 1950 Ford sitting out in front of their house. Some of us thought of asking him to park it in the back but the matter never went very far. It's all right for one of the little fellows at the high school to drive a car like that but a respectable middle-aged man should know better.

It was all black, a four-door sedan, all of ten years old. But it looked brand-new because Mr. Lewisohn had made it his hobby, caring for it, polishing it, and even doing some tinkering with the engine. He would get out on the blacktop Saturday morning and hose that old car and polish it until there wasn't a speck of dust on it, and vacuum the seats and floor. Then he would tinker with the engine. And all that time, for maybe two hours, he wouldn't say a word to anyone except, once in a while, to Mr. Twombley who would be sitting there watching him. If the car got left out in the rain for even five minutes Mr. Lewisohn would get very upset and rush out with a little umbrella which he kept by the door, to put the car in the garage.

Just before he died, Delta made me a present of the keys to my Cadillac which is almost eight years old although it's a 1953 model. But my car is a Cadillac, not a Ford, and I've only driven it about nine thousand miles so it's practically in mint condition, as they say. I've had a lot of offers for my car but I'll never part with it because it was his last big gift to me. So I can see how Mr. Lewisohn felt, in a way; but why did he have to pick one of the cheaper cars?

Some of the embarrassment in the neighbourhood must have got back to the Lewisohns eventually, I guess, because he began to act somewhat strange about his car, leaving it out in front and working on it more and more. And after a while Mrs. Lewisohn never came into the front yard while he was at it. Years ago she used to help him with the car. She might do the vacuuming or clean the windows but as the car got older and older and people began to stare she stayed in back, and finally never joined him at all. When he was up from New York, young Norman was very good to his father about it, kidding him and encouraging him, but even he finally began to seem embarrassed. Norman and his mother tried to get Mr. Lewisohn to spend more time on the garden out back and less on the car. They'd call to him.

'Daaaaviddd!' Mrs. Lewisohn would call. She has a very creaky, what you'd call a grating voice. 'Daaaviddd!'

And Norman would say: 'Come here and bring the trowel, Dad!'

But Mr. Lewisohn would stick his head further under the hood of his old museum piece and pretend he didn't hear them. He'd mumble to himself and bang some tool against a piece of the engine. When they stopped, he would lift his head out of the engine and stare around with his hair sticking up like an old owl. And yet, they say, he was a very shrewd businessman.

My little Mr. Twombley would be sitting out front, smoking to himself, and watching all this, and waiting. What he was waiting for was for Mr. Lewisohn to break down and decide to sell his car. Mr. Twombley was a college teacher – he didn't make much money – and he was pretty hard up for a car.

'Aren't the buses awful?' he would say.

'In West Hartford, Mr. Twombley,' I'd say, 'you're expected

to have a car.' Then he'd pull a long face and mutter something about being 'trapped'. Imagine! 'Trapped' in West Hartford! Most people would give anything to be able to live here. But Mr. Twombley was a restless man.

And so he was watching Mr. Lewisohn, waiting to see if he wanted to get rid of his old Ford. He knew it would be a bargain and he was just a young man; it wasn't necessary for him to have a fine car, just something to get downtown after the buses stopped running at night. He kept staring at Mr. Lewisohn and once in a while they'd speak.

'Have you driven it much?' Mr. Twombley would lead off.

Mr. Lewisohn would peer at him. 'Just around the neighbourhood. It's in better shape than when it was new.' He might have been right at that; the new cars rattle as though they were stuck together with sealing wax. 'Yes,' he'd go on, 'they don't build them like this any more.'

'Jet black. That's the best colour. It's dignified.' He was a smart little fellow, that Mr. Twombley. 'A black car always looks solid and substantial,' he would say.

'Yes, yes!' And the old fellow would stick his head up, running his greasy hands through his hair, looking as though he'd found a long-lost son. Then from the back of the house you'd here: 'Daaavidd! Come along, dear!'

Mr. Lewisohn and Mr. Twombley would exchange disgusted looks and in a few minutes, Twombley would put out his cigarette and come inside, grinning to himself. He knew how to get what he wanted. He watched the used-car advertisements like a hawk, figuring out what he should pay for a 1950 Ford, making notes on the back of an envelope. He finally spoke about it one morning at breakfast.

'One ninety-five. I won't pay a cent more.' I was reading the front half of the *Courant*, not paying much attention.

'It's the going rate,' he said.

'Did you say something, Mr. Twombley?' I knew what he'd said, all right, all right. 'Are you thinking of buying a car?'

He kind of grinned at this. 'In a way ...'

'Mr. Lewisohn's car?'

He looked a bit shamefaced, I don't know why. He had every right to calculate.

'I think he might be ready to sell,' he said, 'almost any day now.'

'I believe you're right,' I said, 'because there's been a lot of talk.' That was at the end of last summer.

All through last fall there were a lot of stories circulating in the neighbourhood, that Mr. Lewisohn couldn't afford a new car, that his business was in trouble, all lies, I suppose. But Mr. Lewisohn looked more and more worried; he talked more and more to Mr. Twombley on Saturdays, when he was cleaning the car, and the two of them got very friendly. From the car, they got on to Jewish literature. I didn't know there was any Jewish literature. And finally, on the Saturday before Thanksgiving, Mr. Lewisohn gave in.

'You have no car yourself, young man?'

'Not yet.'

'Would you like this one?'

'Do you want to sell it?'

'I don't want to sell it but I think it's time.'

'I see.' There was a pause while they looked at each other, each one waiting for the other to set a price. Mr. Lewisohn kept stuttering in a peculiar way.

'What kind of shape is she in?' asked Mr. Twombley.

'She's in good shape. You know that. Do you want to drive around the block with me?'

'All right.' They got in the car and drove off. When they came back around the block you could see that they were talking very fast to each other. They went around the block three or four times. It was hard to keep track of them. I will say that the old car was about as quiet as any car I can think of. Almost as quiet as my Cadillac although I hate to admit it because Delta gave me my Cadillac.

When they got out of the car in front of my house, Mr. Lewisohn put his arm around Mr. Twombley's shoulders; he certainly seemed to like him. They parked the car on my black-top, which I didn't much care for. Some of the neighbours came out to watch what was happening and when they saw the car parked in my driveway I almost expected them to give Mr. Lewisohn three cheers but he went inside right away and Mr. Twombley came inside to arrange with me about parking space.

The neighbours went back inside their houses nodding their heads and talking to themselves.

'What's that car doing in my drive, Mr. Twombley?' I wanted to get my word in first. Delta always told me to speak first when I was driving a bargain, even with my friends, and I've always followed his advice. I could feel him near me right then, so I put my word in quickly.

'Can I rent your other garage?' said Mr. Twombley.

'No, Mr. Twombley, no, I don't believe so. That was the late Mr. Williams' parking space and I don't care to have anybody else using it. It's kind of sacred, don't you see.' He looked puzzled so I kept after him. 'You can park in the drive. Five dollars a month. And you'll have to move your car onto the street before nine o'clock in case I need to get out. Is that satisfactory?' I knew that it had to be satisfactory because there was nowhere else convenient. It was an extra five dollars a month for me.

'That'll have to do,' he said. He was off to New York that night in his car, before they even had the registration changed, and was gone for three days. I believe he had some friends in New York who entertained him royally; they must have been at it night and day for he came back looking like a skeleton. He wouldn't talk about anything but the traffic on the Parkway, which he said was criminal and oughtn't to be allowed; he had been scared by it, not being a very experienced driver. I suspect that he kept talking about the traffic to keep me from wondering what he had been doing in New York.

Mr. Lewisohn bought a new car which he couldn't get used to, no matter how he tried. It had power steering and brakes, and automatic transmission, and he never understood them properly. All the power devices kept getting out of order which meant that the new car was in the repair shop most of the time, costing him money. He had never been a jealous neighbour or a trouble-maker but he began to be very sharp with everyone on the street.

As winter came on, Mr. Twombley came and went as merrily as you please, in the old car. He was never home at night any more, not until one or two o'clock. I would lie awake waiting for him to come home; when he did, he would be singing to himself. Often, he fell down. Then I would hear his key scraping against the lock, or else he would talk to the Lewisohns' dog for half an hour. I never could catch what he was saying but he always seemed to be in a very good humour. He kept on banging up the car, scratching the paint, getting it dirty, and yet it ran and ran as quiet as ever.

In the early mornings, in the winter, he would go out and there would be the old Ford, covered with snow. While he was brushing it off Mr. Lewisohn would appear, glare at him, and go into his garage to try his new car, if, that is, it was back from the repair shop.

Mr. Twombley would jump into the Ford, start the engine – it always started instantly – and move out of my driveway. Poor Mr. Lewisohn had to try and try and try to get his big new monster to go. Often he had to call a serviceman to come and help him. He had big heavy-duty snow tires and still got stuck.

Mr. Twombley went everywhere through the deepest snow with ordinary tires that were worn down to a nub.

They got through the winter without falling out, but when spring came Mr. Twombley was on the road all the time. He just got back day before yesterday from his Easter holiday, just before lunch time and, oh my, you should have seen the car. It was filthy dirty, unrecognizable, and the right front fender and grille bars were waving in the breeze like Old Glory. While we were having lunch he told me that it was mountain-climbing that had done it.

From the corner of my eye I saw the Lewisohns go into the backyard to work on the new flower beds. I hoped that the old man wouldn't notice the car until it was cleaned up and I believe that Mr. Twombley had the same thing in mind although there's no way of telling now, of course. When lunch was over, he changed his jacket.

'Got to take the car in and get it washed,' he said. Just as he went outside, Mr. Lewisohn came around the corner of the house. He went chalk-white as soon as he saw the car and then he began to scream and rave at the top of his voice.

'Robber!' he yelled. "Thug! Bandit! Murderer!' He dashed into his garage as Mr. Twombley turned around, pretty frightened I think, to look at him. Then Mr. Lewisohn came running out of the garage, very fast for a man of his age, waving a spade.

'Murderer!' he hollered again as he caught up to Mr. Twombley. He swung the spade at him, catching him beside the ear. Blood came from the gash. Mr. Twombley fell down and Mr. Lewisohn swung the spade at his head like a golfer. Then he began to run back and forth between the lawn and the old Ford, patting the fender and the grille. Each time, he took another swipe at Mr. Twombley, who was trying to protect himself with his arms.

All the neighbours rushed out and Mrs. Boseman down the block put a rush call to the police who are never, thank the good Lord, very far away. When they came in their cars, the sight of them annoyed Mr. Lewisohn even more. He took one last swing at Mr. Twombley who was unconscious and then charged the policemen, shouting something about their new cars.

They had to take him to jail, naturally, such a respectable householder, and last night, apparently, he had the stroke. Norman Lewisohn is here from New York and he tells me that his father won't live long. It seems that this is his second stroke; it seems that he had a little one to start with, the time he sold his car to the late Mr. Twombley.

The World by Instalments

'HAS IT COME, Mommy, has it come?' chorused Bobby and Jean, joining hands and dancing gleefully around their mother's flowing skirts. Home to their bright cozy box from nasty school they sang for sheer animal joy, fixing their mother above them with swimming grey eyes. 'Has it come? We want to see. Oh, show us!' On they danced and on, dizzying their tall mother with their spinning; her head swam with the rapid circular motion.

'No, babies,' she confessed unwillingly, the poor things. 'Daddy could scarcely pay for the first wall.' As this was clearly an evasion the children's eyes shaded to green at the dismal intelligence and they began to mourn with a keening bitterness.

'Polly and Betty already have all four. They never come out to play.'

They had stopped circling around her; instead they flung themselves, two small rebellious mounds of flesh, on the expensive sod-o-mat lawn. How costly it had been to install over the concrete piazza, remembered Mrs. Thorne, the foot-thick, crease-resistant, artificial lumps had been so heavy! How the sweating deliverymen had groaned as they connected the lumps to the central power unit! And there were still thirty-three lumps of sod to pay for.

She began to consider how she might convert Abe to her way of thinking. Food and shelter were necessities, true enough, but their box, like all the other metal cubes on the interminable block, was mortgaged to the Commissariat of the Interior and they would never be evicted; the mortgage payments could wait. Food was cheap and plentiful and the family did, after all, receive the basic dietary allowance whether Abe worked or not. Her credit at the corner grocery was endless and unimpeachable. She gazed down the block into the distance to where the store reared its cheerful cylindrical aluminoid bulk, like some fantastic silo, against the late afternoon sun. What a comfort the discovery of solar packing had been. Not to worry about food! They could certainly afford another instalment charge, she dreamily realized, half hearing the rebellious wails behind her. Abe would come round, she felt sure. Again, for the thousandth time, she reviewed her astonishment at his funny ways, his tough Yankee refusal to compromise with the realities. She thought of his savings account and his anachronistic cheque-book and began to laugh, feeling her problems melting and becoming unimportant. He could be persuaded; in the end he would pay.

Behind her the keening children raised their forlorn golden heads and examined her calculatingly. They lowered their heads to smother a last factitious burst of sobbing and, silently of one mind, bounced to their feet to tackle her again.

'Mommy will make Daddy buy the other walls,' said Jean to Bobby with her innocent girlish trustfulness, as their mother moved softly towards them. Hearing her child's trusting flattering words, she let an enormous smothering tenderness move in her breast, almost choking her with its palpable weight.

'We *need* the other walls,' Bobby stated masterfully; so like a little man already, his mother confided secretly to herself. Look at him, she marvelled, how commanding, how masculine! She would write a note to Miss Boone, telling her to be gentle with Bobby. She stood and watched them as they continued their curiously adult discussion.

'Polly and Betty got theirs months ago,' said little Jean with a woebegone air.

'Donald has been in the picture since last year,' said Bobby. Their little faces contorted with the effort of reasoning.

'Soon we'll be the only ones on the block without four walls.' Jean took the discussion a step further.

'Then what will happen to us?' they cried, gazing at each other blankly, guessing the answer.

Mary Thorne felt her heart contract with pity as she stood and listened. Nothing should be allowed to bring them to that horrid realization, she vowed, nothing. What had she and Abe done, what had they overlooked, omitted, that Bobby and Jean should have to do without an appliance already so common-place? They shouldn't have to and they wouldn't, she inwardly promised. Aloud she only said: 'Come, chicks,' and led them into their cube.

She opened the instruction manual for their cube-size and showed the children the dining-layout; they gazed at it entranced; it was almost their greatest pleasure to be permitted to rearrange their home. They scooted hither and thither, rolling the storage walls about and unfolding the dining chairs and table. Meanwhile Mrs. Thorne selected the nutrient components from the freezer and fitted them into the de-solarizer compartments, finally setting the de-solarizer on the service board to trans-vitaminize its contents while she waited for Abe.

The children didn't follow the instruction manual exactly; she had scarcely expected them to do so. They trundled the airmetal dining sections slightly off-centre towards the west elevation. When they had everything just as they liked it, Bobby went to the control panel, adjusted the light intake and switched on the wall.

As the atmosphere merged from air-blue through meal-gold to viewers'-green she heard Abe on the sod-o-mat outside. He knocked quietly at the port but she decided to wait until the light setting was homogeneous before she let him through the light-lock. The children, absorbed by the growing figures on the wall, heard nothing of their father's quiet signal. When the correct soft rich tint had enveloped them, they almost disappeared but, alas, not entirely. The abstract illusion which was all the single wall could provide never completely swallowed them. Some final psychical toughness, even in their immature response-organisms, made it impossible to get through with a single wall.

There had been the famous cases, the folk who had managed to become totally absorbed by a single wall. But such cases were extremely rare, as rare as saints and mystics under the older dispensations. That genuine trance, that sinking disintegration into the green light, bringing the utter absorption, could be accomplished by ordinary people like the Thornes only when all four walls were wrapped cozily around them. They were not poor, by any means, the Thornes. Abe's work and his shrewd exploitation of his connections brought them in more value-units than any family on the block. But he was obstinate, her husband, hating to part with his units piece by piece, drop after drop, as was the custom throughout Selenium Suburb. 'At least we own the wall we have,' he told her now and then, and he never made use of the wall, switching it off once in a while over the children's agonized protests and her own muted addiction to the pleasurable illusions moving in the dull glow.

But Bobby! Ah, there was Mrs. Thorne's comfort. She had surprised the lad once or twice when, his sometimes mulish elder sister out of the way, he had applied himself whole-heartedly to their poor single wall. His talent for viewing, talent that perhaps amounted to genius, was tall Mary Thorne's cherished secret. Surprised at his viewing, he had hastily composed himself out of the wavy green and stared at her with clear ingenuous eyes.

'Where have you been, my little man?' she asked him hopefully on one of these occasions. 'Have you been far?' He smiled secretly at her and refused to answer anything except: 'Around.' She worried, poor Mary, that his talent might go for nothing in the face of her husband's refusal to commit himself further. Such opposites, she mused, the dark father and her sweet son. She would have another try.

Inside the cube a rich muted gong sounded quietly, not the magnificent chord of four gongs, but the poverty of the single note; the wall's illusion was complete. She could only just make out Jean's form while Bobby was quite immersed in the opacity. Hearing once more the signal at the port, she switched the inner door tightly shut and waited for the light to alter in the light-lock. Soon it was homogeneous with the inner light and she was able to permit her husband's entrance. Moving with eyes averted around the deepest haze he came to her and spoke aloud.

'Why did you keep me waiting?'

'Hush!' she dictated, putting a finger mysteriously to her lips, indicating the children's fixity.

'What nonsense!' he exclaimed stupidly. 'Look here, Mary, I'm tired of this.' Now it begins, she thought, and hastily moving to avert the possible quarrel she opened the de-solarizer and let the self-spooner divide the appliance's contents. The four neat squares of nutrient tumbled onto their plates, catching her eye as she began to consider how she might talk him round.

'I don't relish coming home to this.'

'No?' she asked, with the beginnings of insolence.

'No! I don't want those kids in there all the time. They're never here when I come home, damn it. I like to see them once in a while. And when they do come out of there, they're bored and silly, and they won't listen to a thing you say to them.'

'Abe,' she cried drearily, 'we don't lead such attractive lives. What can you expect of them?'

'Obedience and respect. And I want them to be able to tell the difference ...' His voice unexpectedly tailed off. Looking uncertainly over his shoulder, he seemed to wonder what to say. But she gave him no time.

'Between the way the pictures are, and the way we live? Is that it?' She had him now, and she wouldn't let him out of the false position.

'The pictures are all very well,' he began, even more uncertainly.

'Abe!' she cried peremptorily. 'The pictures are *official!*' He almost quailed. 'Is there something you don't like about the pictures?' she pursued.

'The pictures are just fine,' he conceded unwillingly.

'And they do the children good,' she followed it up. 'They learn more in an hour from the walls than they'll ever learn from us.'

'I know. I know.'

'Then,' she was going on as he began mechanically to spoon up his nutrient, 'hadn't we better do something about the other walls? The salesman was around again yesterday. He was awfully insistent.'

'You didn't tell me.' He was horrified.

'The children saw him. They thought the new walls would be here today. They were heartbroken.'

'What did the salesman say?'

'He said he was going to give us the other three walls on instalments.'

'No,' said Abe. 'No more instalments. Once you start that they own you for life. Mary ...' His face twitched. 'Don't you see? I can't do that.'

'How much have you got?' she put it to him directly.

'In the telebank? Thirty-seven hundred units.'

'We can pay for two more walls outright. Later on we can get the other one.'

'It took me eleven years to save those units. We'd have no savings.'

'We don't have to have savings. Nobody on the block has anything in the telebank. We can sign contracts as government users.'

'That's no way to live.'

'Everybody does it.'

He tumbled his nutrient about dispiritedly on its tray. 'I don't see why I should bankrupt myself for the pleasure of seeing my children disappear.'

'They're mine too,' she reminded him. 'And I have them around all day. They're pretty hard to deal with.'

'We ought to be able to handle them ourselves. A good spanking ...'

'Abe!' she nearly shouted, horrified. 'You wouldn't *touch* the children?'

'No,' he assented gloomily. 'I guess I wouldn't.'

'We've got enough to worry about without a lawsuit for assault. They'd get a judgement too.'

'I know it.'

'They'd be taken away from us. I couldn't bear that.'

'I suppose you couldn't. I don't know what to do.'

'Well, I do,' she said decisively. 'Tomorrow you can order walls two and three. Bobby has talent, you know. He won't need special training.'

'That's something.'

'With three walls he might do great things. Then you'd be proud of him.'

'I'm proud of him now but I wish he were more like other children.'

'He is like them. He just needs their advantages. Every other child on the block has at least three walls.'

'All right,' he said, suddenly badgered into it. 'I'll order them tomorrow. And pay for them too. It'll take every unit we've got.'

'We'll always be taken care of.'

'We ought to take care of ourselves.'

'Oh, Abe! You're so old-fashioned!' But she had gained her point and she gave him a special treat for dessert, some vegetables grown in the ground. She looked at him with disgust as he wolfed them down.

'I don't see how you can eat them. Those nasty green leaves.'

'You don't know what you're missing.'

'I'm just as glad,' she said.

What hustle-bustle, what comings and goings about the Thorne cube on the following Saturday! There had never been a Saturday like it within the remembrance of poor Abe Thorne who lay sleepless listening to the joyous shouts of his offspring and their buddies. Out on the sod-o-mat the neighbourhood children leaped and cavorted, singing gleefully, as they waited for the exciting great grey truck, the morose impersonal deliveryman, the two additional walls for the Thornes' set.

He felt guilty: all along the interminable block their friends and neighbours, or at least, thought Abe glumly to himself, Mary's friends and neighbours and the children's, had known about his intransigence, and had reprehended it loudly, with mighty affirmations of the value of having everything everyone else had. He had fancied, as he glided along the escalade to and from the helistop, that each family in its forbidding cube watched him and eyed him and silently commiserated with his long-suffering wife. 'That poor girl!' he could imagine them saying to each other, and: 'Does he think he's worse than everybody else?'

Worst of all, it dragged property values down if someone on the block let his property go to seed. One was expected to have at least three walls. If you didn't have three or four walls you could move to one of the dark tenements in what had been the centre of the city – that dreaded deserted place, that monument to a society irretrievably destroyed, existing now only for the outcast, the mad, the marginal. The public library was in the centre of the city, and the municipal institutions, and he would be a brave man who frequented the town meeting or the lions on the steps.

Long ago, before his marriage, he had yielded to his tall slender sweet fiancée's demands and given up his solitary flat in the centre of town from which, at night, he had been accustomed to go walking, picking his way over the huge stones and mounds of rust, remembering how it had looked when he was a little boy. He had wanted to go on living there but she had dissuaded him.

'You couldn't bring a child up there. Only think ...'

'I guess you couldn't,' he allowed, though he couldn't see why; *he* had been brought up there. 'But we don't have a child.'

'We will soon,' she'd told him, blushing charmingly. 'In about five months.'

'Oh.' Then he thought of something. 'Whose?'

'Do you remember Charlie Brewer?'

'Yes.'

'His.' And at his look she had gone on. 'Darling, you took forever to come to the point.'

'Yes.'

'Darling, you don't mind, do you? You're not going to be last-century about this, too?'

'No.'

So they were married and they took the embryonic Jean – he always thought of her as Jean Brewer somehow – to live in Selenium Suburb. They had been quite happy but he had never forgotten the look of the moonlight on the stone blocks downtown.

Outside the shrilling baby chorus rose and rose. He heard the grinding of gears, the motor of a heavy truck; that would be the deliveryman with the walls. With a sigh he got up, put on his uniform and went, telecheques in hand, to the door. In the living area the heavy wire connections had already been bared, leaving a mess of metal stripping all over the place. The servicemen were locking in the walls and as he watched them he was aware of the hard cold stare of the deliveryman. Feeling more and more under surveillance, he turned to face the man.

'Shall I pay you now?'

'Depends,' said the man in a surly growl. 'How many walls do you want to pay for?'

'You're mounting two and three, aren't you?'

The serviceman spat disgustedly. 'You'd better get a move on, Buster. I don't like coming back here time after time. You gonna take the fourth wall?'

'I can only pay for two.'

'Forget about paying.'

'But I want to pay as we go.'

'You sound like a radical to me.'

'No, no, no, nothing like that. It's the way I was brought up.'

'Forget the way you were brought up,' said the man. 'Take the fourth wall. Pay me for two today and I'll put in the other one on Monday. You can take a government loan contract.'

'I'll pay for two and think it over.'

'All we want to do is put them in,' said the serviceman. He laughed. 'Once they're in you're stuck with them.'

Young Bobby had been eavesdropping and as the lowering serviceman turned away the little lad accosted his father with an equally menacing scowl. 'I think we'd better have all four,' he said.

'Oh you do, do you?' said his father exasperatedly. 'Well just you march right outside, young fellow. You're getting in the way.'

At length the hammering and banging stopped and Abe began to think of returning to his warm bed. He paid for the installation, ruefully contemplating his depleted chequebook, and when the men finally departed he stared around the room at the vast expanse of innocent-looking grey glassola. There was no telling, he reflected, what might develop out of the walls. So perfect was their broadcasting orientation that they responded to whatever mood the viewer projected. The live multi-dimensional figures that emerged from a single wall usually imposed their own story upon those who watched. But with three walls, and a certain imaginative capacity, and a perverse moral capacity for acquiescence in the nearly real, the viewer could impose his own story on the dramatic universe. He wondered about Bobby, wondered what sort of dizzy world his gifted but erratic son might dream out of the glassola.

Behind him the noise of childish revelry and holiday had stopped; the silence deepened. He heard the closing light port, heard it lock securely behind him, and knew that his three dear ones were surrounding him to assist at the trial. He turned to look at them and was amazed at the transformation. The least entranced was little Jean, obstinate, mulish, and yet in some ways the most intractably human of them all. Charlie Brewer's child. She stood looking; oh, undoubtedly she was eager. She was all readiness to test the walls but yet she showed a hard unwillingness to succumb to them entirely, right out of hand. Tall sweet Mary, his wife, seemed quite possessed by the splendour of their new possession and the rosy future it promised of numberless appliances. Her face was swept by dreams as it had been when they had fallen in love. She gazed first at the walls and then at her best-beloved, her Bobby.

And he, Bobby, was vibrating like a dynamo; he positively hummed with his divine electricity, so ready to impose his talented image-making mechanism on the world of the walls. His head rotated back and forth almost mechanically like a spectator's at some celestial ping-pong tournament. He was a taut greyhound straining at the leash till all at once his mother loosed him; then he sprang to the light intake and the light began to green, to go deeper and deeper green, until they were sunk, crouching tightly, in the bath of light.

Never before had the Thornes moved deeper into the light, the submarine richness that folded around them. They tried at first to keep an eye on each other but the attempt was useless; there was too much green. It grew and grew as they sat on wondering whose illusion would appear, knowing in their hearts that if any one of them could dominate the shadow-world of the glassola, it would be Bobby. There was fear then in the mind of each as, all at once, the green began to part, and emerging rounded figures came to life among them. Spiky plants which flowered uneasily into unusual blossoms sprang out of the soil around them; huge leaves waved lazily above them. It was a jungle world whose people at first seemed pygmies. As the Thornes sat waiting, preparing to take their parts in the emergent drama, they could feel an alien element, a certain falseness in the values of this particular world.

Those who came to them first were silent, tiny, and rudely misshapen; their hands were crabbed, their heads twisted and knobbed, their bodies seamed and old. They ran crazily from one of the elder Thornes to the other, singularly avoiding their juvenile creator. They looked beseechingly up at the great Thornes, Abe and Mary, who sat bewildered on their metallene stools. The tiny dream-folk attempted speech but no sound came despite the dreadful importance they seemed to attach to their attempt to cry and demand.

Time sped until at length all four of the dreamers knew that the illusion was defective. It was no good, this world. They willed it hastily away and faded back through the green to the daylight.

'You stopped me,' Bobby wailed as they stared at the bare living area. 'You don't want me to get through. You hate me. Oh, you hate me,' and he glared defiantly at his father.

'No, Bobby, no,' his mother flew to his side. 'You'll have the other wall Monday.'

'I will, Mommy? Promise?'

'Yes, darling. We've waited too long as it is.' And that was how it was accomplished.

When the children returned from school on Monday the affair was complete. Four shining expanses of glassola greeted their shining eyes and they danced, holding hands, around their mother's skirts. 'It came,' they bubbled. 'It came. *We* must try it now, before Daddy comes. We'll surprise him.'

'That's right,' said Mary. 'We'll give him a surprise.'

From the very first they sensed the difference, even the obstinate Jean whose sudden approach to puberty sometimes obscured her understanding of these mysteries. The light was more warm, more rich, than ever; the set hummed peacefully, introducing Bobby and his mother to a mild repose. 'How right, how natural it is,' murmured Mary as the swarms of tiny dream people waltzed happily around her skirts. She stood and began to examine their figures more closely. They were, she realized with a shock, all males. Despite their size they were not children but seamed and lined little men, frightened, and still consciously avoiding their creator who now rose and took the centre of the stage like a tragedian.

His mother gazed. He was ten times the size of the cowering men, the frightened dark pygmies. Her Bobby beckoned; in the dream she came, brushing through the hordes of minuscule gibbering savages; she clasped his hands. And the tiny men began to describe in complex circles the dance steps of a propitiation. There was no more green now, but a clear living atmosphere, a new world in which as she came to herself she moved willingly, submissively, to the altar.

In clear shrill wails the little men pronounced their prothalamion.

When Abe came home that night, the doors of the cube lay open. From inside, he realized acutely, there came cries, the cries of a single voice. He raced inside. On the floor, full-length, sobbing in total rejected bewilderment, lay Jean. 'I couldn't get through,' she wept. And then: 'They've gone.' He took her up gently.

'They won't be back,' He faced it with her. 'We must do, you and I, what we can alone.'

The Glass of Fashion

PORKY VALENTINE had always worked in the communications industry which is a tough and romantic field, and very glamorous. But despite the glamour he had always tried to prevent himself from being drawn into the sweeping tides of fashion which revolutionize the customs and manners of that industry, at work and play, several times a year. He had done so from the very beginning. To begin with, he had not gone to an Ivy League school nor to Hollywood High and UCLA. Coming as he did from the Mohawk country in upstate New York, he had gone to St. Lawrence, where the chief sport is ice-hockey, if you can imagine. The college had been a second home to him; he had never regretted the fact that few people had heard of his Alma Mater.

After graduating in the early thirties he kicked aimlessly around Watertown and Utica in a variety of petty jobs, none of which gave him any pleasure, until he became an announcer on a local radio station with a nominal network affiliation. The station carried very little network programming. Instead the staff concentrated on local-interest shows done live and in this kind of work Porky exhibited a certain flair. Most of his time was taken up by the hack-work – the midnight-to-six stuff – that falls to the lot of all junior announcers. But he also began to put little programs together and to learn production values. After he produced and starred in 'Porky's Pigs', a fifteen-minute show devoted to livestock prices, he began to attract notice in the larger centres because of his liveliness and originality. He moved on to Albany and finally, just as the war broke out, to New York.

He always regretted missing the war, as he might regret missing a hit show or the St. Lawrence-Queen's game; but his punctured ear-drums kept him in New York where he did mighty important work on morale-building home-front sustainers. He got much valuable experience in his war effort. The end of the war found him, at thirty-three, settling happily into his bachelor's life as a Greenwich Village apartment dweller.

In one of the communications media, you stand to learn all about what is most up to the minute – or even a little before the minute – in taste. After all, even the most advanced public opinion must be taught what it likes, by means of radio, TV, and the magazines. Porky understood this. He was able to see how he and people like him in a tiny enclave of taste and judgement, of which he was at the centre, formed and developed the habits of hundreds of millions of people. He accepted his responsibility with a certain awe as he moved higher in the production echelons. The more he saw, the more he resolved to keep his own ideas and his own taste independent. He wasn't, he vowed, going to be led by the nose like everyone else.

He was glad, for a while, that he had gone to St. Lawrence. He felt that his cultural matrix, as he called it, the regional background that he'd found upstate, was quite unique. He spoke of this, with a good deal of modest pride, one day at lunch, to a couple of Yale men from the staff of another show.

'St. Lawrence, eh?' mused the elder of the two. 'That's curious. I always had an idea you'd been at Yale.'

'Not me, boy. I'm from the heart of the Iroquois country. Mohawk, Oneida, Onondaga,' he chanted, 'Cayuga, Seneca, Tuscarora. The Six Nations.'

'That so? I went to Georgetown myself. Did you know that Georgetown is the oldest Catholic college in the States?'

'No,' said Porky, idly.

'Well, it is. It has a great tradition. Back in 1798 ...'

'I went to the University of Akron,' said the third man loudly. They all began to talk at once and ordered another drink.

All afternoon in the studio Porky felt sleepy and a little resentful. He wondered why Bert Fallon had thought he went to Yale. The question stayed with him all the way home but he forgot about it when he looked around his apartment, admiring the way the decorators had followed his instructions. There were the low flat couches and the butterfly chairs. The mobile by a friend of his at the New School. A de Kooning that had cost like hell. Walls and ceiling in peach, chocolate and burnt orange. A garbage disposal. It was his own and there was nothing, then, quite like it.

He hadn't yet discovered that there was a terribly expensive Jackson Pollock hanging back-to-back with his de Kooning in the adjoining apartment. He was pathetically fond of his cozy apartment.

He liked it the more because lately as he got older and maybe, though he wouldn't admit it, rather lonely, he began to sour a bit on his work. Well, not his work, exactly, but the people it linked him to. He hadn't been in news and public service for some time now. Instead, he was doing adult drama, a half-hour once a week from eight-thirty, and thinking about moving into TV as soon as it got rolling. His show was sound as an apple, he knew. He had a big enough budget and he had learned that it was wise to spend all that could be spared on good scripts.

All the same, there was something about his show and the business generally that griped him. It wasn't so much the sadists and queers; you had to take them for granted. It wasn't even the way the really good writers and musicians (he felt that he could still recognize the good ones) had trouble marketing their stuff. There was some overriding thought-control. Something that made everybody act alike.

He had found out by this time that his early upbringing and education did nothing to make him special, unique, or free, so he began to take thought for the morrow. He considered his apartment. It was good enough, he supposed, as it was. Anybody in the u.s. would be glad to live there. You saw ones like it perpetually in the slick home magazines. In fact, an acquaintance of his, a very unusual fashion photographer, had wanted to use it for a magazine piece.

'I can't let you use it, Jake,' he had protested. 'I don't want my place being imitated in Superior, Wis.' But he knew then that he'd have to get rid of it.

'I think you're just an old meanie,' said Jake. 'It's such a darling place. Heavenly heavenly de Kooning. It's just right for the book.'

'That's what's wrong with it. Oh, hell! Do the piece if you like; but don't use my name because by then I won't be living here.'

He was very restless these days and so he began driving out deeper and deeper into Connecticut. It was only in the last year of the forties that he definitely decided to make the leap. That year TV mushroomed dangerously although it had been stealing top men from radio for years. Porky had been sitting on the sidelines watching the others going over the fence – the sheep – one by one. He knew that he'd have to switch sooner or later but he wouldn't jump because everyone else had done so.

There was an additional, somewhat more realistic, reason for caution and delay. It was a one-chance-and-out affair, the big jump. Many of his friends had found out to their cost that they couldn't learn television technique on the job, the way they had in radio. The public, that monster in Superior, Wis., had become accustomed to the split-second perfection of timing which radio had taught them. People expected TV to have the same smooth surface. Plenty of good men had struck out their first time up; now they were making the rounds trying to get another chance without too much response, without even much opportunity of getting back into radio, a medium which they understood. Radio was drawing in its horns in the face of terrific competition from the baby giant.

So from 1947 till 1949 Porky sat on the sidelines like Charlie Conerly, confident that he'd get his chance, wanting to take the chance at the right time, and extremely anxious not to waste his impact on the wrong situation. And all that time he was turning over and over in his mind his personal situation and hidden dissatisfaction. It all boiled up in him finally as a result of a chance conversation over a five-o'clock drink with Ed Tcherny, his assistant producer.

Ed had been going like a house afire in news and documentary for the other net until the day, three years before, when he'd stepped into the top slot on a TV half-hour – he hadn't even lasted thirteen weeks. Two and a half years later he got another job when Porky, who liked his work and admired him personally, took pity on him and gave him an opening. Ed was talking slowly while he nursed a drink and waited for his train.

'You see, Porky, you can't learn it from the book. Because there isn't any book. You have to be very nimble.'

'It makes no difference if you're good?'

'Everybody's good. They're all good. You know most of them.'

'It sounds like roulette.'

'It isn't that the boys aren't smart. Inventive.'

'What is it, then?'

'Well, you can't afford to be good, original, offbeat. In radio, yes. Once in a while. Not in television. You have to stick to the format.'

'Why?'

'Porky, I honestly don't know. But I'm glad I moved out of town. It nearly killed me.' Then Tcherny grimaced bitterly and wouldn't say any more. He finished his drink and caught his train, leaving Porky to make up his mind. He did so then and there. He'd get out of town, way way out. Not like Ed, who'd only gone as far as Redding Ridge. Way out ...

In a few months, at the end of the autumn, he found what he'd been looking for, up in the northwest part of Connecticut, almost up to the Massachusetts border. Eight miles from Canaan, the nearest town. There was wood on the property and the house, as far as he could tell, hadn't been touched. Certainly it hadn't been painted for fifty years and the wall planking had that pure silvery sheen that wood gets when it weathers soundly. There were two rooms and, believe it or not, outside plumbing, and, a decent distance away, a well. He paid what he considered a really modest price and moved in. It was terribly cold, the house was, and he made no concession to the cold, cutting his own wood from his own brush.

Five times a week he had to drive at breakneck speed eighty miles southeast to the Parkway and on into the city. He didn't mind a bit.

He had five acres, almost all wooded, and there were only one or two overgrown paths along which he'd sidle happily to cut brush for the fireplace. One day towards Christmas he was swinging his axe with his usual inefficient but mighty stroke when he heard 'chunk chunk chunk' right nearby. At first he thought he owned an echo but then he realized that there was someone near him, also using an axe. He pushed through the brush until he saw it begin to move and heave; and all at once the woodcutter straightened up and looked at him.

'Howdy, neighbour,' said Porky, with that fine stubborn New England taciturnity; then he turned to go.

'You're Valentine, aren't you?' asked the man with the axe. 'I'm Blasingame. Horton and Blasingame, you know. We used to have the CHEQUERS billing when you did a nighttime seg for them.'

'Oh.'

'That's right. Can you come over at five? Madge will want to see you. She's left *Vogue* and she misses the city desperately.'

'Sure,' said Porky.

'Wear a sweater. We're going to have to enlarge our fireplace. Just half a mile up the back road. I guess we're in deeper than you are.'

'I guess you are.'

He went over at five and at nine o'clock had sold his place to a friend of Blasingame's. Next Monday he was back in the city holed up in a suite at the Plaza. He began to arrange his affairs with the same fierce desperation he'd developed driving back and forth across Connecticut. Right after New Year's he finished his arrangements. He was through with radio, or nearly through, for there was only the spring season to survive and next fall he'd be in TV where a whole new life seemed to beckon to him. There'd be no format stuff – the network assured him of that. He'd have an absolutely free hand; the more creative originality he could bring to the job, the better.

Knowing there was only the spring to get through kept him more or less alive and happy as he severed his ties one by one. He wondered what to do during the summer and listened constantly to the views of his associates: some were for European travel; one man was going on a dig among the Pueblos; others had picture commitments; cruises to exotic lands were offered weekly in the newspapers; he might stay in the city and research his fall show. None of these alternatives excited him; he thought of going to the Lake Champlain country and canoeing but it was too much like Grossinger's. And so on.

At length he heard something that interested him. He was talking affably enough to one of the network messengers one morning. The lad was fresh out of college and happened to mention his vacation just before his senior year. He had worked for a mining company which held some base-metal leaseholds in Labrador.

'They flew me in,' said this boy. 'To a lake. There's a million lakes up there. I went with a prospector named Alex Murray. He was the only person I saw all summer.'

Porky was transfixed. 'What did you do?'

'I'd go out by myself every morning. I had a geology hammer. Once in a while I'd knock a chunk off a piece of rock.'

'What were you looking for?'

The messenger laughed. 'I never did find out,' he said.

'And you only saw one person all summer?'

'Well, once we met an Indian. God knows what he was doing in there.'

'Why,' said Porky, 'that's a wonderful way to spend a summer. I think you've given me an idea.'

He gave the lad a friendly encouraging pat on the shoulder and stepped out of the elevator headed towards his final production meeting. That morning the atmosphere of petty chicanery, throat-cutting, and career promotion seemed peculiarly repellent but Porky was able, for the first time in months, to shrug it off lightly. He listened to the complaints and appeared to give them his fullest consideration. But all the while he was imagining a sheet of quiet water and a soundless canoe and perhaps a dour Scot in the background. Later in the day he made extensive enquiries, bought a map of Canada, and forgot about the bullies, perverts and sadists. Let them, he thought, let them go and make their movies. I know better.

In early June he flew off to Canada, travelling light and planning to buy what he needed when he got where he was going. He wouldn't go to Labrador; the messenger had been there. So he stopped in Toronto and checked over a list of suitable places. He decided easily enough that Algonquin Park, an enormous tract of virgin country in Northern Ontario, was the place to go. Guides were available, he was informed, and there were so many lakes that he could have his pick for his own personal use. He left for the north in a small chartered seaplane and put down twelve hours later on a lake which he had selected purely arbitrarily by pointing a finger from the air.

The pilot seemed disturbed. 'I can't leave you here alone,' he said.

'I've got equipment for the night,' Porky said. 'I want you to fly to the nearest town, hire a guide, and tell him to buy only the things we'll absolutely need. Guns, a canoe, tackle.'

The pilot looked at him dubiously and then, seeing that this was what Porky really wanted, he was kind and flew off.

Porky watched the sun go down, rejoicing. Then he made himself a frugal meal, with the most extraordinary difficulty. He passed a violently uncomfortable night, being totally unprepared for the myriads of aggressive flies. He rejoiced again. Early in the morning the plane returned through a blue and orange glory bringing the guide and the equipment. His name was Alfred Big-Canoe. He had made extensive purchases, many of which seemed superfluous to Porky. He gazed with special distaste at a battery-operated portable TV.

'Take that thing back to town,' he told the pilot while Alfred stared in silent protest. And giving the pilot money and instructions about his monthly return, Porky sent him away, cutting himself off for good.

'What are we going to do?' asked Alfred.

'Make a camp. Sit.'

'That's all?' with dissatisfaction.

'Fish a little.'

'Lake fished out,' said Alfred gloomily, but he helped make camp, somewhat clumsily. They sat and smoked, saying nothing, and a great peace invaded Porky's soul. For the first time in years he really relaxed.

The days passed dreamily in discomfort varying from moderate to acute. They patched the canoe and then patched it again, endlessly. Porky became used to the icy water around his knees. He loved his lake.

'What's it called?' he demanded of Alfred, one day.

'I dunno. Too many lakes.'

'We'll call it Mirror Lake,' said Porky. He looked down into the clear still water, gazing at his mirrored reflection. 'It's the only name.'

The seaplane made the first and then the second of its monthly visits. Each time the pilot stared curiously at Porky and each time seemed pleased with what he saw. Porky was by now the colour of an old well-cared-for highly polished brown shoe. They made definite engagements for the final visit, gazing deeply with a fine honest candour into each other's eyes. They were men of the air and the wilderness together.

'I'll be back,' said the pilot. 'Sharp on time.'

And the last three weeks sped past. The unbroken solitude had soothed Porky to the point of somnolence and he went about all day in a drowsy peaceful snore. He and Alfred made an amateurish survey of the lake, making many rough sketches on bark. They knew all its eddies, its moods and depths. They did not go too far up or down the rivers which fed it, or which it fed. He didn't want to know where they came from or where they went. Late in the evening in the last week of their stay they were up river half a mile or so when from some little distance, not far off, they heard singing and the echo of voices:

'Ohhhh, when I get a couple of drinks
    on a Saturday,
Glesga belongs to me. Toooo mee.'

'I wonder who that is?' said Porky half to himself.

'Tourists in next lake,' said Alfred. 'They wanted me for guide but you pay twice as much.' Then they paddled back to camp.

Two days later the seaplane came, early in a drizzling dark morning. They sank the superfluous equipment, Alfred appropriating what was still valuable, and flew to town, where they bade the guide goodbye at the landing. Porky gave him an outdoorsman's grip, a firm handclasp. Then he and his friend the bush-pilot flew back to Toronto.

The next morning he was back in Manhattan, refreshed and ready to work as never before. He was cleansed, eager, with his creative imagination at a tautly productive pitch. It was like that all the way through the first and part of the second week on his new show. But as he watched, and learned his new trade, and tried to keep his feet, he realized suddenly and sharply that all the bullies, plotters, and perverts were tanned the colour of old shoes and were going around exchanging clear candid stares and frank and manly handshakes.

Marriage 401

MICHAEL DIDN'T ARRIVE in the coffee shop until nearly
three o'clock, when he and Rosemary had a class together. He
had had a busy morning rehearsing *Pullman Car Hiawatha* for
the drama festival and then, after lunch, there had been the exhi-
bition of Nigerian carving at the museum. His mind was still
busy with his impressions of the weird slab-sided masks, their
grotesque appearance to his eyes, and their sharp evocation of
some sense of religious mystery. He could remember quattro-
cento faces of Christ which betrayed the same weird angularity.

When he came into the room he could see that Rosemary,
JoAnne, and Bert were at a further stage of their year-long
debate; they looked like the masks. They were waving their
arms in a familiar nervous pattern: cigarette smoke hung over
the table. There were at least eleven dirty coffee cups in front of
them. Before he joined them he went to the counter and, staring
inattentively at the display of pennants, T-shirts, and stationery,
emblazoned with DESAULNIERS in block lettering, he
ordered coffee.

'Better make it four cups,' he told the counterman. 'Stand
one on top of the other.'

'How's it coming, Mike?' asked the counterman.

'All right, I think. We might win.'

'I've sold a lot of tickets over the counter.'

'The more the better. How about it, Paul? How long have
they been sitting here?'

'Since I came on at noon anyway. Here's your coffee.'

'Thanks,' he said, balancing two cups precariously in each
hand, a trick he had learned working in an all-night restaurant.
The cups were of cheap thin plastic and began to hurt the palms
of his hands before he moved away from the counter; once he
nearly dropped them. The others saw him coming, stacked the
empty cups and made a place for him. Bert took the empties
back to the counter.

'How can you drink so much of this stuff?' he asked the table
at large. 'It's unspeakable coffee.'

'It's terrible,' said Bert mournfully. 'I'm so dizzy from drinking it that I've missed three classes.'

'I've missed two,' said JoAnne, who followed Bert's lead in all things.

'I haven't missed any,' said Rosemary virtuously, raising her eyebrows. 'I haven't had any yet.'

'Why didn't you come to the rehearsal?' he asked her. 'We were on stage for the first time. I worked out the light cues.'

'It's bad luck,' she said gravely. 'Like seeing your bridegroom the morning of the wedding. I don't want to give you bad luck.'

'I've got all I need.'

'How's Claireen?' demanded JoAnne tactlessly. She was always deliberately tactless; it was the major aspect of her social face. 'Is she co-operating?'

'Claireen feels' – he thought it over – 'oh, she feels that the collegiate theatre should be like the professional theatre in all respects, should set as high a standard of performance, should do important plays. Therefore' – he drew a deep breath – 'she puts her theory into practice by being as indecent, foul-mouthed, and abusive as she believes all leading ladies must be.'

'Are they like that?'

'The professionals? Not at all! In my experience they're uniformly polite and docile. They'd never put a director through the paces Claireen does me.'

'Why don't you get rid of her?'

'Because she's the best actress who ever came to DESAULNIERS. Am I speaking in block lettering? It's those crests and pennants.'

Desaulniers was one of those large urban Catholic universities which had begun existence as Saint Somebody's Seminary. With the growth of the city in the nineties, the founding fathers had adopted the name of a French explorer of early America – to give the university a kind of neutral public appeal. Now, throughout the metropolitan area, all public fund-raising campaigns, newspaper releases, and civic pronouncements treated the university like any other great civil institution. The ecclesiastical connection had been subtly played down in the establishment of its public image; important research in rubber synthetics had been concluded by the department of chemistry. The university was co-educational, had a large lay faculty and was in every respect indistinguishable from any other similar institution, which was what the founding Fathers had likely had in mind. Desaulniers had now reached a pinnacle of native American security, of *indigeneity* (the word was a coinage of a sociologist in residence) which permitted it the luxury of a losing football team.

The four students looked for a moment at the array of block-lettered crests behind the counter.

'Gracious!' said Rosemary. 'How they do abound, those emblems! Why do you suppose it is?'

'The search for a native cultural identity?' JoAnne had read this somewhere, or picked it up from Bert.

'We have a quite sufficient identity,' said Rosemary impatiently. 'If only somebody around here recognized it.'

'The Order is no good,' said Michael.

'They're the root of the whole trouble,' said Bert. 'They want us to be good little Americans like everybody else. Courses in cosmetology! There's an Americanism if you like.'

'It's almost exclusively an American congregation,' said Michael. 'They haven't had the advantage of European scholarship. They're more ultramontane than the Vatican civil service.'

'They've no scholarship at all,' said Rosemary.

'They're anti-scholarship and anti-liberty. They're instrumentalists.'

'What does that mean?' asked JoAnne.

'Take the Ecumenical movement,' said Bert largely. 'Take modern Biblical theology. Take theology in general. In America Catholic theology is moribund, a corpse, rather, a tissue of exegesis of Aquinas. There's no life in American Catholic thought.'

'Oh, for God's sake!' Rosemary took it up. 'Look at their attitude to sex!'

'They got that from the Jansenists,' said Bert glibly.

'We hear such a lot about the Jansenists,' said Rosemary, rounding on him. 'But whoever made the connection clear?'

'All the Irish clergy from the seventeenth century on were educated in France,' said Bert.

'Can you prove that?'

'I think so. Why?'

'I don't think it's Jansenism at all,' she said. 'Or rather, Jansenism is only part of the larger picture. I think it's an attitude common to a certain type of Catholic thought from the beginning. All the Latin Church fathers warn the girls to wear turtleneck sweaters – loose-fitting ones – and skirts down to their heels.'

'I didn't know that.'

'Sure they do. You can find it in Salvian. Or look at Jerome. "A married philosopher is a contradiction in terms."' She thought of something else: 'What do you suppose the Wife of Bath was bitching about?'

'I wouldn't buy a blanket condemnation,' Michael said cautiously. 'Many theologians aren't disturbed by the functions of the senses. Aquinas depends on them for a great deal.'

'Of course,' Rosemary amended. 'He knows that the senses are from God and so are the delights of the senses. But you'll hunt a long time before you'll find an English-speaking priest who feels comfortable with a drink in his hand. Unless, that is, he happens to be English. And when it comes to sex – well, look at this next class. 'Marriage 401.' What does it say in the catalogue? – 'Studies in the marriage contract and its intricacies. Head and heart interaction. Domestic economy and marriage-partner functionalities. Readings in the appropriate Papal Encyclicals.' Only some celibate neo-Thomist or some progressive educator could write prose like that.'

'Extremes meet,' said Michael. 'They're very much alike. It's the attempt to systematize life out of existence.'

'Certainly it is,' said Rosemary indignantly. 'None of these men would say "Shit!" if he fell in it. And yet they offer courses in marriage-partner functionalities.'

'You might as well give a course in beef stew or Martini-mixing.'

'Sure!' she said. 'You don't *think* about marriage the way you think about the syllogism in Barbara. I doubt if you can be said to *think* about it at all.'

'How do you think it should be approached?' asked JoAnne timidly, quailing before Rosemary's bluster.

'By going to bed and getting children and caring for them,'

said Rosemary and as she said it she looked Michael squarely in the face, daring him to call her bluff.

They had been warring over the contradiction between her sexual professions – her doctrine – and her actual frigidity for close to two years. She meant well, he supposed, but like them all she wouldn't, or probably couldn't, lay it on the line. 'Put up or shut up,' he thought to himself but he said nothing to that effect. Instead he said: 'Let's go to class. You've been sitting here long enough.' She bridled at his proprietorial tone but came, as he had known she would.

'I won't offer to take you to supper,' he said, on the way to the third floor. 'I can't afford it this week.'

'I'll take you,' she proffered.

'No, you won't,' he said automatically. 'I'll call for you at seven and you can watch the dress. You can keep an eye on Claireen for me.'

'I'll keep an eye on Claireen for myself,' she said. 'I don't like the way that girl jiggles and bounces.'

'All actresses bounce.'

'Marriage 401,' she said as they went in the door. 'Isn't it silly? It's the wrong time of day anyhow.' They sat in the back row, not to hold hands as many young couples did in a kind of endorsement of the aims of the course, but to preserve and fortify their attitude of critical detachment.

Today the priest who taught their section was introducing the subject of contraception, which embarrassed him so acutely that he waltzed gracelessly around and around his main points like an itchy performing bear. He, Father Mahaffy, that good grey man, had the one defect that the lecturer should at all costs avoid. He put you quite to sleep, not with his line of thought, but with a certain droning quality of the voice, a soporific bass tone impossible to resist.

As its name and number implied, 'Marriage 401' was a course for seniors given in eight sections of which Father Mahaffy's was the least popular. Michael and Rosemary had asked to be assigned to him because they respected the good old man and liked him; they attended loyally out of pity for his obvious fish-out-of-waterness. He had originally been trained at Louvain and the Collège de France as a rational psychologist and teacher of ethics and this assignment had come as a bit of a shock. He rather floundered in his discussion of the physiological aspects of the subject; phrases like 'the intromission of the penis' fell drearily flatly from his lips. Rosemary and Michael guessed that his soporific drone was being cultivated in this class in an attempt to persuade the young ladies present to ignore the awful things he had to say. He bored his other classes unpremeditatedly.

'Let me put it this way,' he floundered now, to his class's amused inattention. 'Suppose you had seven babies and only six hats.'

The class was willing to suppose this for the sake of peace.

'Very good,' said Father Mahaffy, pleased that no one had challenged him. It was a working assumption of the group that they all knew more about 'life' than the lecturer. 'Very good! Now which would you do? Cut off one of the babies' heads? Or try to find a seventh hat?' He seemed to think he had an open-and-shut case but the class hung fire on the answer. Halloran, a contentious red-headed radical who sat in the front row, was ready now with his stumbling-block.

'Doesn't your argument assume, Father, that the seventh hat is absolutely, metaphysically, unavailable to begin with? And don't you then go on to withdraw the assumption? In which case you haven't really been restricted to six hats at all. I don't believe your metaphor fits the facts.'

'How do you mean?' asked the priest hopelessly. His harmless illustrations were always riddled by Halloran's logic.

'Well,' said this *advocatus diaboli*, 'the proponents of birth control by artificial means teach us that there is an absolute outside limit of supply – in short that we reach a point where the seventh hat simply is not going to be available no matter what our efforts to find one. Do we then bring the baby into the world to starve?'

'I'd have to question their figures.'

'Why? Food supply is limited. Population increase is not.'

One could safely ignore this. Michael glanced at the clock; it was a quarter to four. Putting out his hand he touched

Rosemary's wrist tentatively but she shook him off and went on conscientiously taking notes. She planned to present a typed set of her notes to Father Mahaffy at graduation, believing that he would be helped to marshall the course better with a set of student reactions at his elbow – he might write a textbook and mention her in the preface. So she shook off the caress, glancing at Michael and winking. He went then, as he had planned from the start, into the slumber with which he habitually beguiled the last ten minutes of this class.

'How are you coming with those notes?' he asked her when they were again free, moving downstairs in the crowd.

'Great,' she said, laughing. 'The things that poor man says. I don't believe he knows how awful he's being. Listen to this: "The female is much harder to arouse and infinitely harder to appease." Where in the name of God did he find that?'

They laughed together and went out into the sunlight, crossing the campus towards the women's residence. Once again he took her hand and again she shook him off.

'Just a minute,' she said. 'I want to put on my mittens.'

At the door of the residence, an imposing Georgian affair whose denizens, according to Rosemary, herself not excepted, laboured in the last stages of neurotic decay, they paused for a moment and reviewed their night's engagements.

'Are you sure I can't take you to dinner?' she asked wickedly.

'I'll tell you how it is,' he said. 'I've enough money for one good dinner with drinks, or two poor dinners without.'

'I see.'

'There's no point in spoiling one good dinner.'

'Very true.'

'I'll see you at seven. We have the use of the stage from seven-thirty till ten.'

'It's a dreadful play. I don't know why you chose it.'

'It has lots of body movement. And that's all the cast can handle.'

'All those wrigglings and writhings. They don't add up to anything.'

'They don't have to for the effect I have in mind. We're going to win the drama festival this year.'

'Why didn't you choose some nice rational art-form like architecture?'

'Manichee!'

'I suppose so,' she said. 'I'll see you at seven.'

He was able to squeeze out three drinks at dinner which got the evening off on the right foot. As they were to be working in the theatre, Rosemary had tightly girt herself in a pair of ballet tights, eluding the nun at the door by wearing a skirt over them. At the theatre she would discard the skirt and appear correctly attired for the evening's strenuosities. She would have made use of a cigarette-holder, purely out of a perverse sense of satire, but Michael talked her out of it.

'The tights make your point,' he said. 'For God's sake don't give Claireen the idea you're making fun of her.'

'Why not?' she asked innocently.

'She'd walk out on us. She takes her art seriously.'

'She'd be no great loss.'

'I warn you. I'll make you take the part yourself.'

'Nothing to it,' she said. 'Wait till I get my skirt off. Anybody can jiggle her buttocks.'

The female is harder to arouse, thought Michael as they crossed the park to the student union. I wonder if she's really harder to appease? He was beginning to think he'd never find out.

The rehearsal was funny. With her hair in a frowsy pony-tail, her deliberately cultivated pigeon-toed walk, her air of mad innocent inconsequence, Rosemary was the perfect parody of all undergraduate enthusiasts of the drama. She stood, ostensibly helpfully, in corners handing people things at the wrong time, saying little, subtly being in the way. He knew what she was doing and why – skirting the borderline which, too obviously crossed, would make their leading lady scream like an angry chicken. All Claireen knew, in some dim way, was that she was being kidded; she couldn't work up a specific charge.

'Did you have to bring that bitch?' was the only luxury she permitted herself.

'Now, Claireen,' he said, harried. 'She's a fresh reaction.'

'Michael dear, if she doesn't waltz her cute little ass off this stage she'll get a reaction from me and it'll be goddamn good and fresh.'

'Rosemary!' Michael called. 'Would you go to the back of the house and check the voice levels for me? I want to see if everybody can be heard.' With relief he saw her turn from chucking a stagehand under the chin and march off through the darkened house.

'That's a good girl,' he called.

'I can hear that,' she called back and the rehearsal went on. *Pullman* is a tricky play to stage but at the end of two hours Michael was approximately satisfied.

'All right, everybody,' he said at length. 'We're on last tomorrow night. I'm calling the crew for seven. I want the cast in their dressing rooms, made up and in costume, by eight forty-five. Got that?' They all had it and the rehearsal was over.

After their coffee – he let his stand and cool and finally go unconsumed, he was sick of coffee – he walked her back to the residence. She had her skirt on again, he noted, and he began to think that maybe Claireen had a point at that. When, at the lowering neurotic gateway to the residence, he tried to kiss her good night, and when she twisted away from him as usual, his irritation finally overflowed.

'That isn't what you want,' she said sweetly, virginally, twisting away. It was what she always said.

'Do you know what I like about you? The only thing I like about you?' he whispered. 'I've just figured it out.'

'What?' she asked breathlessly, ready for a compliment.

'Your bottom,' he spoke good and loud. 'You have the nicest little pair of buttocks I've ever seen. Nicer than Claireen's even. I'd like to use them for a pillow. I'd like to take a great big bite out of each cheek.'

She was all wounded, invaded, threatened, going dead white and then crimson. 'Nobody ever said such a thing to me in all my life,' she gasped. 'You're disgusting. I don't want anything more to do with you. Don't phone me because I won't answer.' She turned and ran.

So that's that, he thought as he walked off. I wish I weren't ever going to see her again. He knew that he would, of course.

The Triumph of the Liturgy

CLARE AND HAWLEY MEGAFFIN are going to the ten-ten
this morning, and taking the baby, which means considerable
inconvenience for themselves and anyone in their immediate
neighbourhood in church. Whenever they've tried bringing
young Tom before this it's always ended in either Clare or Hawley, or both, fleeing in dismay carrying a squalling infant and
trying to ignore the steely glances of the ushers.

Tommy is only eleven months. It isn't that the Megaffins are
trying to force his religious education before he's ready. But
they are tired of going to church separately – it's a dreadful nuisance – first one slides out to the early Mass and has to leave
directly after the Communion so the other one can be on time.
They can't have breakfast together, spending two or three hours
over the *Tribune* and the *Courant* as they used to. Technically
the parent who has to remove the baby during Mass usually
misses one of the principal parts of the service and, again technically, that parent has missed Mass.

The Megaffins hope and believe that the Lord will overlook
the technicality; and off they go to Saint Justin's with Tommy
clutched in Clare's arms, already annoyed at having been
crushed over-hastily into his snowsuit.

Saint Justin's is an enormous parish and the church is packed
at every Mass on Sundays. As a matter of fact, the Masses are
doubled, with two going on contemporaneously in the church
and the parish hall in the basement. The one in the basement
starts ten minutes after the hour to accommodate the chronic
latecomers among whom are the Megaffins who are always in
aisle seats in the last row, or standing among the crowd in the
vestibule.

With masses at eight, nine, ten, eleven-thirty, eight-ten,
nine-ten, ten-ten, and eleven-forty, and a full house at every
Mass, with so many people going to Communion, Monsignor
Wahl has a traffic and logistics problem, and a shortage of staff.
It is a source of continuing and acrimonious debate among the
pastor and his assistants at what hour they should run the High

Mass. The only time it can be fitted in is either eleven-thirty or eleven-forty but the 'late Mass Catholics' who arrive at that hour are always unmistakably eager to get home to their frugal breakfasts of Bromo-Seltzer, tomato juice, and hair of the dog. So the pastor has hesitated to detain them. On the other hand, the choir and choirmaster are indignant that their services are passed over lightly in the parish, except for the occasional requiem for a stockbroker, and Midnight Mass at Christmas.

Then too the sermons have to be pared down to the minimum running-time, otherwise, with the number of regular communicants, the Masses run overtime into the next scheduled hour and conditions become chaotic. What with one thing or another you can always expect to find Monsignor Wahl (who says his Mass privately at six-thirty) hopping around like a cat on a griddle, upstairs and downstairs, trying to keep his schedule running fairly smoothly. During the week he spends much time scouting for extra clergy to say a Mass or help to distribute Communion. And the assistants are complaining that they can't do justice to their sermons in seven or eight minutes.

Nothing happens around the plant – he calls it 'the plant' – that Monsignor Wahl doesn't know about. He built the church, the rectory, the sisters' home, the school, the garage and parking lot, himself, starting in the depths of the Depression, and the parishioners agree that he has done a marvellous job of digging the parish out of debt. And they are right and he is justifiably proud; there isn't a plant like it in the archdiocese.

The Megaffins are not surprised, then, to discover their pastor pacing up and down in the basement vestibule when they come in. They aren't surprised but they *are* a little frightened. Even though Curtis Megaffin, Hawley's dad, has been a mainstay of the parish for thirty years, Hawley is still somewhat in awe of the pastor who shouted at him when he was preparing for his First Communion. Also, the pastor is averse to infants at Mass and has been known to peer down from the pulpit and order an offending baby from the building. So they sneak quietly by hoping he won't notice them, immensely surprised to find that they aren't late.

Well, not *very* late! The Mass has progressed no further than the Gloria which is very unusual, for it is already ten-thirty, or even later. The church, or rather the basement, is jammed and if the regulars all go to Communion Monsignor Wahl's schedule is in trouble, which explains his preoccupation in the vestibule. What, wonder Clare and Hawley, can be the delay?

The reason is soon apparent. During one of his lightning forays to the cathedral, on the lookout for stray clergy, Monsignor Wahl has invited a young Maryknoll Father out to Saint Justin's to celebrate Mass and to give the sermon today. He is to speak at as many Masses as he can conveniently fit in, on behalf of the missionary activities of the Maryknoll Fathers, and he is celebrating the ten-ten in the basement.

The long low-ceilinged hall is stifling as usual and, again as usual, it is dangerously overcrowded in contravention of the fire marshal's agonized directions. The Megaffins take their place among the crowd in the back and begin to hand Tommy back and forth to one another, a routine which they hope will keep him approximately placated for a while. He seems less restless than usual; the crowd bothers him less and he stares at the altar with round, nearly comprehending, eyes, almost seeming to understand what is going forward. And there does seem to be a significant difference in the order of proceedings on this particular Sunday. The congregation is quieter than is customary, whether from boredom or mere preoccupation or enthusiasm for the liturgy, it's hard to say. But certainly the young missionary is taking things a lot slower than do the harried parochial clergy. He reads the Latin as if he understood it and it meant something:

> *Munda cor meum ac labia mea, omnipotens Deus, qui labia Isaiae prophetae calculo mundasti ignito:*

From an inspection of their missals, the Congregation are aware that this means:

> Cleanse my heart and my lips, O Almighty God, who didst cleanse the lips of the prophet Isaias with a burning coal:

Something in the behaviour of the missionary – is it his diction or his intensity? – makes the time-worn phrase, seen every Sunday since babyhood by all present, come meaningfully alive. In short, he seems to mean it. The altar boys, unused to this pace, scurry here and there self-importantly with nods and bowings and bobbings at the knees, as though they were saying the Mass and the priest were holding them up. Having been used to the zip of the parish clergy (especially Father Curley who can rip one off in thirteen minutes) they try to speed things along, being aware of the pressing necessity for despatch. In fact, one of them, Jack McDermott, son of our biggest local undertaker, undertakes to let the priest know by means of a whispered phrase at the gospel side that he is holding everybody up. All he gets is a cool stare for his pains. At length, before the congregation has become too restlessly inattentive, the gospel is read and the young priest crosses to the pulpit to implement the annual plea for funds of the missionary society.

This, now, is a ticklish business. Any member of the secular clergy will tell you that the continual solicitation of funds is the most irksome and humiliating of the priest's duties. They hate, naturally they hate, to be bringing the matter up every Sunday, but what's to be done? The fire marshal says the school must have two new fire escapes and two sets of doors chopped in the walls. This will cost fifty thousand. Taxes must be paid, and insurance, and fees to the organist, the choir, the sextons. Gas costs something and the priests can't do their job without transportation. So many sick calls, so many to be visited, work in the hospital, and all the other routine matters, and where's the money to be had? Then there are the irregular and the regular annual diocesan collections for one purpose or another, and every purpose an excellent one, for the Holy Father, for Catholic University of America, for the new high schools, the Easter collection for the Archbishop, a testimonial to a departing assistant. All good things!

Monsignor Wahl hated to ask for money when he was a curate. When he became a pastor he had to get used to it but it still bothers him after thirty years. He stands at the back of the church to see how the young Maryknoll father manages his request, to see if he can coat the pill sweetly enough.

In the pulpit the young man is even more deliberate than

before. He first identifies himself and the congregation stiffen their spines against the pews; they know what is coming. And they know too that each of them will take the proffered envelope home with him, think about it through the week, and give something, a little less perhaps than might be managed, but something.

The speaker uses no high pressure come-ons. He tells his story, tells about the work of the order, says that he too hesitates to beg but that it must be done if the work is to go forward, and finally assures the parishioners that he places his confidence and trust in them and that he will offer his Masses and prayers for their intentions. He is very quiet, very restrained, very convincing. He makes us feel uncomfortable about our contributions as we sit there; are we really doing as much as we can? It is an example of what is called, in other quarters, 'the soft sell'.

The monsignor listens and nods with approval; if it has to be done this is the way to do it. He wonders to himself if there is any way he can estimate the results and then remembers that his own staff will unseal the envelopes and send a cheque for the total to its destination. He makes a mental note to record the result and then, examining his watch, realizes that it is past eleven and there is still half a Mass and the serving of Communion to go.

'Get them in and out quick,' he reflects. 'I might as well be running a restaurant.' And of course in a super-substantial sense, he is. Anyway he wishes he could speed things up a bit and he goes to the sacristy to vest himself in alb and stole. He will help to distribute Communion and have a word with the celebrant.

He is alone in the sacristy rummaging in a closet for a spare stole and can hear the strong clear low-pitched voice outside, respectful of the words it is saying. Last night at supper the young chap has told the pastor and the assistants something of his experiences during the last days of his mission on the Chinese mainland. Toil, want, envy, malice, sickness, imminent danger of imprisonment and possible torture, possible death or disgrace, all these things have fallen to the lot of the young chap while he, old Monsignor Wahl with his papal prelacy and his wealthy parish, the crying babies, the young families and the late-Mass-Catholics, have been prospering at home. He knows why he sighs to himself.

In the pews, along the aisles, and at the back, the congregation is stupefied with boredom and restlessness; they are unaccustomed to passing so long a time on their knees and cannot find thoughts to fill their heads. Trained by years of habit to recite mentally a dozen prayers learned under the Sisters in the parish primary school, or to read inertly their missals, or just to sit, they cannot pray in any different sense. Once in a while perhaps it crosses their minds that the service has some meaning beyond what they have been taught and half forgotten; but they had all that in the primary grades and feel no necessity of going through it again. The study of ritual is third-grade stuff.

Hawley Magaffin, though, is in a slightly different case from the majority of his friends and neighbours who fill the hall. At one time, like most of us, he considered the priesthood as a possible choice of life. This was when he was in college, a little younger and less well informed about the world than his classmates. He picked up certain phrases about the 'way of perfection', read a book or two and often fancied that he was marked out for a more active religious life than his buddies. He went on dating though, Clare and other girls, and at length found himself in the position of being an engaged man. He still can't say precisely how this happened. One day he wasn't and the next day he was and there hadn't been anything *said* that he remembers. Still, there it was: they had a pleasant quiet wedding in Utica with only the immediate thirty relatives and two hundred and fifty selected guests present. Then there was the baby and by now, in his lawyer's office and at home there seems no reason why he should annoy himself with these unrealized ambitions. After all, he thinks, you shouldn't think of your religious life as something you make a success of. Success is irrelevant here.

Besides he is a considerate husband and the kindest of fathers and this, he believes, will count for something. We can't all be heroes. It is sobering reflection of this general order which makes it possible for Hawley to endure and even to enjoy the laborious course of the service which now, to the unfeigned relief of everyone else present, has reached the Communion. The parishioners flock in their usual large numbers to the altar rail; it makes a nice Sunday morning routine. Up at nine-fifteen, church at ten-ten, breakfast and the papers from eleven-thirty till the middle of the afternoon. But none of them will be home by eleven-thirty today.

Down from the altar comes the missionary and behind him the pastor who grabs the second ciborium hastily and rushes to serve his half of the communicants. Monsignor Wahl resembles, most of all, a one-armed waiter at a soda fountain during the lunch-hour rush. He is supposed to enunciate a certain phrase aloud as he gives each soul the wafer. But years have eroded the phrase and what comes out is:

> *Corpus donner noster Jesu Christi casto nommen tuum vitam ermine. Men!*

The other priest is travelling back and forth at half the speed and what he says is:

> *Corpus Domini Nostri Jesu Christi custodiat animam meam in vitam aeternam. Amen!*

'Preserve my soul unto life everlasting,' muses Hawley Megaffin as he approaches the rail on the gospel side, inching forward most slowly because this is the missionary's side and progress is slow. The pastor is giving Communion to three times the number and when the two priests meet at the centre of the rail, as once or twice they do, they gaze blankly at each other. In his heart Monsignor Wahl is remembering all the times he has sweated for three hours in a confessional with sixty sinners while in the other box across the church some nice-Nelly newly ordained youngster is hearing two, patting the transgressors on the head and burping them. It seems unfair.

The two men reascend the steps to the altar where the young celebrant wipes and re-wipes the sacred vessels, the Monsignor kneeling, boiling with impatience, at his side. At length the tabernacle is shut and as he leaves the altar the Monsignor gives the missionary a meaningful stare which, translated, means: 'People are waiting. Hurry up!' But he doesn't attempt a translation, going serenely on his way.

The congregation hang on grimly, wondering how long he can manage to drag things out. Wonder of wonders, at the very back of the hall young Tom Megaffin is fast asleep in his father's arms, a thing which has never happened before. Passing the young couple as he returns to his agitated stance at the rear, Monsignor Wahl espies the sleeping child, smiles approvingly – there's a well-trained baby – and pats Tom on the head to the pleased bewilderment of his parents who have expected the opposite reaction, if any.

The ushers are lined up at the doors preparing to distribute envelopes for the parishioners' Maryknoll contributions. They do not expect to be stampeded by any concerted rush, the service has lasted so very long. Now at last the priest concludes the Salve Regina and the Prayer for Peace and the congregation leaps as one man to its feet, genuflects hastily while the priest is still on the altar, and begins to crush its way outside.

They have been thinking things over in the last hour and a half, so it would seem, remembering the old days, the very old days, when a sinner might be required to spend six months in ashes on the steps outside the church before receiving absolution. An hour and a half really isn't so bad. Some of the oldest parishioners can remember when the service was always as long as that. They're getting off easily, they seem to concur; so in spite of their boredom and annoyance at the untoward delay they snap up the proffered envelopes and think about them seriously all the way home. What's a couple of dollars?

Let Hawley Megaffin serve as our emblem! Why, he decides as he inserts the envelope in his missal as a marker, why, we're not doing too badly! He wonders about the size of his contribution, deciding to talk it over carefully with Clare when they get breakfast on the table and the papers spread around on the floor.

The following week the collection returns total the astonishing sum of thirty-eight hundred and fifty-seven dollars and change. Monsignor Wahl is made most seriously to reflect; Hawley and Clare have made a small but genuine act of self-denial; in another city three hundred miles away the young missionary develops his argument anew. Things are looking up liturgically.

Which the Tigress, Which the Lamb?

'HAVE YOU HEARD, dear Dr. Bledsoe,' demanded Mother Mary Mechtilda of that inoffensive gentleman one day, 'have you heard about Betty Brokaw?' Her wimple arched with static electricity as she waved a newspaper clipping before him.

He confessed that he had not.

'Examine this document, if you please.' She handed him the clipping, a photograph in fuzzy grey tones. The inaccurate reproduction typical of the daily press confused him, and he found it difficult to establish the subject of the picture and its inflammatory aspects. At his side, Mother Mary Mechtilda jiggled on her heels, her robes swishing around her.

'We are responsible,' she said, 'wretched, wretched girl! Abandoned child! And after all I admitted her to the college and you are her faculty adviser.'

Closer perusal made the photo seem clearer. Lined up on some sort of runway or platform were three girls in skimpy bathing suits, each holding a basket of flowers, and each with a curious ribbon depending from the shoulder athwart the *poitrine*. Bledsoe had to squint to make sense of it. There were these three girls, sure enough, but how did Betty Brokaw come into it? He scrutinized the caption:

JAYCEES NAME MISS WENTWORTH COUNTY: Jayne Brokaw, centre, 21, an honours student at suburban Mount Mary College, carried off top honours in last night's runoff. Flanking her are runner-up Elspeth Cabot, 18, left, and third-prize winner Sandra Lyauty, 20, right.

'Who is Jayne Brokaw?' he asked in bewilderment. 'Is *Jayne* a Christian name?'

He had given the *ay* the correct diphthongal or Latinate pronunciation, and she made haste to correct him.

'It's pronounced "Jane",' she said. 'That's the way they spell it in the movies.'

'I see,' he said, but he didn't.

'There's more besides,' groaned Mother Mary Mechtilda, 'there's a newspaper story.' From the inner recesses of her robes she produced a second piece of paper, handing it to him to read:

HONOURS STUDENT REIGNS AS MISS WENTWORTH COUNTY

JAYNE BROKAW PERFECT THIRTY SIX

'I want to be a model or an actress,' said newly-crowned Miss Wentworth County of 1964 Jayne Brokaw as she was led to the winner's enclosure at Civic Stadium last night. 'I've studied Elocution and Poise, and I'm ready for any proposition.'

The comely Jaycee Queen, 21, holds first-class honours in Economics and Business at Local Mount Mary College. While training as a statistician, her own vital statistics of 36-20-39 have proved more important in her young life. She hopes to enter films if her present prospects mature.

One of a family of eight children, Miss Brokaw has been employed in the summers in the secretarial pool at DOSCO. Next step in her blossoming public career will be the province-wide Miss Ontario contest to be held next week in Kingston. Victory there can mean an eventual invitation to the Miss America Pageant at famed Atlantic City in September.

While Dr. Bledsoe figured this out, Mother Mary Mechtilda watched his face for signs of recognition, growing more and more impatient as none came.

'It's her,' she exploded, 'can't you see? It's her, stark naked.'

'It is she,' said Dr. Bledsoe automatically and then, recollecting himself, 'who is it?'

'It's Betty,' the registrar sniffed, contumeliously. *Jayne* Brokaw indeed, the little snip!'

'This?' He indicated the central figure, all teeth, hair, skin, legs, arms. 'This is Betty?'

'It is indeed. She's your advisee,' she reminded him.

'It doesn't look like the same girl,' he stammered, and he stared harder and harder at the photograph, the tossing long apparently blond hair, the peculiar banner across the swelling torso, the puff of flesh at the edges of the drum-tight square-foot of bathing suit. 'Are you sure?'

'Look at the face!'

'It's all blurred.'

'It's the same girl, all right. I didn't know she was an honour student.' It was a delicate point for a registrar, he could see. 'I've examined her standings,' continued Mother Mary Mechtilda, 'and she was telling the truth.'

'How do you mean?'

'About her standings. I can't vouch for her other statistics.'

'I expect they took measurements of some kind for the purposes of the contest,' said Dr. Bledsoe painfully. Here the class bell rang loudly and he seized the pretext and beat it, still carrying the clippings. He had no class scheduled at this hour, but trusted that the registrar might not realize this. Alone in his office he mopped his brow feverishly, flattened the clippings on his desk, and tried to order his thoughts. 'His advisee.' 'Their responsibility.' He shuddered, in great distress of mind, as he considered matters.

MOUNT MARY COLLEGE was neither large nor widely known, so that it was with grateful relief that James Bledsoe had accepted his appointment to its faculty some years before. His unimpeachable credentials, his Toronto PH.D., had procured him a period of secluded uninterrupted meditation, and he was therefore able to pass his days in a dreamy contemplation of public credit, the bank rate, the business cycle, and the gradual decay in the stability of the currency – for he was a Coynian by temperament – with no pressing sense of involvement in business or affairs. At some propitious moment he hoped to launch the fruit of these meditations upon the world of scholarship in the form of a fat tome whose title alone had exacted months of excogitation:

PRICE INDEX AND WAGE SCALE FALLACIES:
Being some account of a systematic enquiry into iso-
morphisms believed to exist between all conceivable
models of economic universes and the real behaviour
of money in circulation; together with a short history
of the Coyne affair, and a re-evaluation of the appli-
cation of probability theories to prediction of consumer activity.

If this title was overpowering, the book was calamitous, or
would be when his opponents had had a chance to examine it.
Then, and only then, he had trusted, would he exchange the
cloistral calm of his daily round amongst the Sisters for the acri-
mony, indeed the outright throat-cutting of learned contro-
versy. He had prepared himself an arsenal: graphs, interviews,
pamphlets, back issues of *The Canadian Forum*. At no time had
he envisaged the possibility of being drawn into other arenas
than the scholarly. But now this extraordinary conduct of Miss
Brokaw threatened to bring public witness, public contest,
crashing in on him. He had taught her statistics, among other
things, and profiting from her statistical researches, she had
learned to profit from a statistical isomorphism with her own
conformation. '36-20-39.' Was it a norm of some sort, he wondered? What was the accuracy of the sample? Was there a mis-
representation curve?
    He weighed the evidence before him. She had plainly done
something to her hair, and the face just wasn't there. There
remained only the totally unfamiliar evidence, which he had
never seen in the three-dimensional round and which he never –
God help him – wanted or expected to see, that is to say, the
long slender beautifully shaped legs, and the delicately rounded
arms, and the rest.
    He would accept the evidence of the caption. If the *Spectator*
chose to assert that this was his Miss Brokaw, he would take it
on their authority; but what an ominous set of differentiae! *His*
(for he thought of his students as 'his') Miss Brokaw had never
raised her voice above a submissive murmur, nor raised her eyes
above the level of her secretarial notebook. He knew nothing of
her grades in merchandising or typing or office management,

having left these matters to less superlatively qualified members of the department. He had had her only in Advanced Statistics, Money and Banking, Economic History, and The Business Cycle, and in each of these she had been the same quiet child, with the same mouse-coloured hair (what had she done to it? — he was innocent of the uses of a blond rinse), the same dun-coloured sweater and skirts, the same noisy big boots, and never a word to say for herself, and an honours student, and had she been planning this for four years?

Twice a year he had interviewed her in his capacity as her faculty adviser and she had never shown the slightest interest in any other career than a modest secretarial post which might lead to an assistant office managership. Once only, he remembered now, had she dropped a handkerchief between them and when they both bent to retrieve it a heady scent had been wafted up from, he believed, the front of her sweater. She had prettily apologized as their heads bumped, and now she was Jayne Brokaw, and Miss Wentworth County, and there remained the prospective news from Kingston and possibly even Atlantic City!

DOWNSTAIRS among the filing cabinets in the registrar's office, that functionary was being cross-examined by her chief, the President of Mount Mary College, Mother Mary Prudentia. They conversed in muted tones, canvassing the unfortunate situation from all angles.

'We can't expel her,' said the registrar. 'The creature has done everything asked of her academically.'

'Moral turpitude? Conduct prejudicial to Mount Mary?'

'It won't do, Mother, we'd never get away with it. There's the press to consider, what with the building fund drive and all. Have you discussed this with Mother Bursar?'

The President acknowledged that she had.

'And what does Mother Bursar say?'

'She says that Miss Brokaw has paid her fees. She says to be very careful.'

'I believe she's very wise.'

'Yes,' admitted Mother Mary Prudentia with reluctance, 'but you saw that photograph. Have you ever in your life seen anything to equal it?'

'No.'

'Nor have I.'

'What will his excellency say?'

'Oh, him!' exclaimed the President impatiently. 'He's hand in glove with these Chamber of Commerce people. He'll laugh, if I know him. He's a man, after all; he won't understand.'

They put their heads together and the rest of the conversation proceeded in secretive whispers. As the President took her leave, she tossed her head with a gallant fillip which, many years ago, had made her the most adored and imitated fifth-former at Marymount Academy, the idol of the baby class, the delight of the sisterhood.

'That Dr. Bledsoe,' she fluted high-spiritedly, 'he thinks of nothing but figures.'

She went back to her office to brood.

The next week was punctuated by a series of peculiar phenomena, phone calls from scandalized alumnae, jocular notes from gentlemen members of the board of governors, satiric messages from other sisterhoods, all of a remarkable character. Far from suggesting horror or revulsion, these communications unanimously bore witness to widespread (if horrified) interest in their champion, and a buoyant hope that her career might progress unimpeded to the final apotheosis at Atlantic City, N.J., and Hollywood, Calif.

'It says in the *Spectator*,' remarked Mother Mary Mechtilda to Mother Mary Prudentia at breakfast some days later, 'it says here that these contests are conducted on two levels, the level of talent and the level of beauty.'

'I see,' said the President with an unwonted grimness. 'What, precisely, are Miss Brokaw's talents?' Suddenly, surprisingly, she bubbled over with laughter.

'She intends to recite a speech from Shakespeare's *Henry V*,' said Mother Mary Mechtilda, 'the one beginning "Once more into the breach, dear friends."'

'At Atlantic City?'

'No, she still has to win at Kingston.'

'She'll win at Kingston all right, I'm certain of it.'

'If I may say so, Mother President,' said the registrar tentatively, 'you don't seem too unhappy about it.'

'Aileen O'Connor!' exclaimed the President, using the registrar's baptismal name for almost the first time since they had been fifth-formers at Marymount forty years ago. 'Don't be a silly goose! Whether we like it or not, this girl has manufactured a strong position for herself. I don't like it. I think it indecent and a wretched example to the student body. And I must say, I think Bledsoe has let us down. But there it is. She's going to win; I feel certain of it, and we might just as well put up with it.' She thought it over far-sightedly. 'Who knows, it might not be a bad thing for the college publicity-wise, I mean. What with the building fund drive just getting started.'

Dr. Bledsoe had likewise passed an uneasy week estimating the probabilities of Miss Brokaw's triumph at the intermediary, or Kingston, Ontario, stage of her development, and like the President, he found them high, too high, and both were speedily vindicated in their judgement. Friday night Jayne carried all before her in a kaleidoscope of bathing-suits, rose petals, flash-bulbs, muttered curses from lesser beauties, and floral horse-shoes marked SUCCESS.

An independent producer shooting a picture at Niagara Falls offered her a walk-on. The offer was at once accepted, the scene was shot, processed, shown to the press in Buffalo, Hamilton and Toronto, cut from the final film as had been the producer's intention from the beginning, and a great deal of free publicity for his dreadful film and for the fledgling star was conveniently obtained at very small cost to any but the patient subscribers to a number of Ontario dailies.

The next week, Miss Ontario officiated at the christening of a motel in Clappison's Corners. Two nearly infant children who were observing the event from the higher boughs of convenient trees fell out of them, crashing to the ground and achieving multiple fractures. The proprietor of the motel was sued for two hundred and eighty-five thousand dollars, under the 'attractive nuisance' rule.

The managers of the Miss Ontario pageant announced their intention of backing to the hilt the candidacy of Miss Brokaw at the late summer passage of arms in New Jersey. Enthusiasm was running high, province-wide.

A bemused faculty, a sisterhood beset with wonder and

annoyance, observing these goings-on with ears to the ground (which always produces a false perspective) wondered and waited for word from above. The president of the student government, a startlingly unmemorable child, was known to feel keenly in the matter; her enemies were persuaded of the riot of an envious gripe in her bowels, and were likely right. The faculty, in silence and in secret, cursed the Department of Economics and Business, and the Department of Economics and Business, more silent still, cursed James Bledsoe.

Each day Mother Bursar reviewed the takings in the building fund drive, and found them good.

In his shady sunlit office, Dr. Bledsoe perceived that his work on his book was not progressing satisfactorily. Now it was summer: the recent graduates had departed. Summer school had begun and only the very stupid failures from the previous term, plus a host of dogged high-school teachers, filled the halls. He offered no courses to such as these, feeling that the summers were his own to spend in research. But the genuine scholarly stillness about the heart, the meditative indifference to things of the senses, was somehow harder to achieve this year. He couldn't focus on theories of invariance; when he passed nuns in the corridors they eyed him peculiarly. He dug morosely in his enormous green filing cabinet for material collected what seemed an age ago, spread it on his desk, and was unable to understand it, distracted by whispered rumours in the halls.

The end came swiftly. One morning a purple Cadillac twenty feet long appeared in front of the Administration Building and then disappeared as silently as it had come. Then there was a grotesquely speedy visit from three high dignitaries of church, city, province, unscheduled, intolerably out of the way. Then there came a remote crew from the neighbouring TV station intent on getting several hundred feet of usable film.

'CTV News,' they said when quizzed. 'Background on the story.'

'What story?'

They wouldn't say. There was much talk about Pierre Berton, but he never showed. In a week she was to leave for the boardwalk.

The next Tuesday morning at 10:05, Dr. Bledsoe was frightened nearly out of his wits by the enormous sudden blaring out of sixty band instruments in a cacophonous version of 'A Pretty Girl is Like a Melody'. Putting his head out the window, he saw the three high dignitaries, the Hamilton Fire Department Silver Band, the purple Caddy with Miss Brokaw straddling the recessed top, hundreds of crepe-paper streamers, a beaming Mother Mary Prudentia carrying a miniature Mount Mary pennant on a stick, three TV cameras, and a great many other people and things, all trying to fit themselves through the door of the Humanities Building in a lump. He had a crazed feeling that they were coming after him, like a mob in Baroness Orczy. This impression was much heightened by the increasing noise of the band, and the sound of feet on the stairs.

They were on the second floor – and then the third – and coming along the corridor. The door of his office flew open and they tumbled in, first a clutch of photographers, then the three dignitaries and Mother Mary Prudentia; then they carried Miss Brokaw in on their shoulders. The noise was inconceivable.

'Put her up there!' everyone shouted, and in an instant she was perched side-saddle on top of the enormous filing cabinet, grinning down at them. Flash bulbs exploded. Somebody thrust a miniature Mount Mary pennant into his hand. He waved it. He could make out Mother Mary Prudentia hollering 'Good luck!' in a stentorian baritone. Then they all took up the cry, all but those who were singing or chanting.

With a mighty sweep of his arm, James Bledsoe swept the surface of his desk clean and leaped atop it, waving his pennant with one hand and conducting the band with the other. The chorus rose and rose:

'Good luck at Atlantic City.'

'Success.'

'Hooray for Jayne. Hooray for Mount Mary.'

A hundred and thirty typed manuscript pages of a book on statistical models and consumer behaviour were trampled to indecipherable shreds by the feet of the mob.

'Hooray for Jayne. HOORAY.'

'HOO!!'

Presents for an Anniversary

MADDY AND KATH were talking outside the open window so Paula listened casually; they were only children and could have nothing shameful to conceal.

'They have secrets all the time,' said Maddy with indignation. She has a hard sense of social protest unusual in so young a female. 'I don't think it's fair.'

'Who *has* secrets?' Kath has a trick of emphasizing the unexpected word, sounding as though she means more than she says.

'Old people.'

'Which ones?' Kath went on bouncing her ball against the wall of Paula's apartment, thump thump thump; she'd been asked not to do it.

'All of them.'

'So do we. Why not?'

'But they can always guess ours.'

'How do they know?'

'They watch us.'

'We'll watch them.' Kath is very matter-of-fact.

'I do already.'

'Who?'

'Mummy and Daddy.'

'Do you guess their secrets?'

'No. I can't tell.' Then she must have grabbed the ball.

'*Don't* do that!' Kath said with a shriek. 'Maddy! DON'T! It's my ball.'

The scuffle lasted a moment or two. 'Damn you, Maddy! I was up to thirty-five.'

'I've done much more than that,' said Maddy calmly. 'Mummy's going downtown today.'

'You're crazy.' Then interestedly: 'How do you know?'

'She's mending a hole in her gloves, the blue ones.'

'She must be, then.'

'Yes, I think so. I was born four years before their wedding anniversary.'

'Four years *after*,' said Kath, stressing the right word for a change. 'It couldn't be before.'

'Why not?'

'It couldn't. It's always after. I was born two and a half years after. So I'm a year and a half older than you.'

'And Sandra's the youngest,' said Maddy, with deep satisfaction. 'That's a good thing.'

'For you.'

'Yes. Why doesn't she tell us when she's going downtown?'

'She'll tell us.'

'She might not, some time.'

'If she's going, she'll tell us.'

'She might not get back in time for supper.'

'She always does.'

'But she might not.'

'Well, I don't know,' said Kath. 'She always has.'

'They talk with their heads.' Maddy was plainly very put out about something.

'With their mouths.'

'No, their heads! So we can't tell what they mean. Daddy turns his head like this,' she illustrated it, 'and Mummy doesn't say anything. And then they look at each other. *I* know. *I've* watched.'

'Mummy always has tea at G. Fox's when she goes downtown. They have little sandwiches, round ones with cheese, green and orange.'

'Why does she want to go downtown? She hasn't asked what I want for my anniversary.'

'It's their anniversary. It's your birthday.'

'How can she know what I want if she doesn't ask me?'

'Oh, bugger!' said Kath loudly. Paula choked back a giggle. 'The ball's gone into the flower beds.'

'If they catch you in the flower beds you'll get a spanking,' said Maddy blissfully.

Kath's voice floated up from the lawn below the porch. 'Get me a stick, Maddy, a long one. I'm going to poke it out.'

'You'll break the tulips.'

'No, I won't. Hold on to my legs.' A suspicious silence followed during which Paula could imagine the havoc being wrought in the superintendent's carefully tended floral borders. He passed his life away chasing children around and around the huge old house.

Suddenly from above there came a stern shout: 'Maddy, Kath! What are you doing? You know what I told you. Run away from there!'

'We're not doing anything.'

'You're in the tulips.' It was remarkable, Paula thought, how clearly a voice carried from the third floor.

From the lawn, desperately: 'I can't reach it.'

'Mummy's coming,' said Maddy coldly. 'You're going to get it.'

And from above: 'You're both going to get it.' There came a thundering descent of the stairs, a tramping as of armies, as Mrs. Gauvreau swooped from on high, sailed past Paula's half-open door out on to the lawn in full pursuit of her offspring. There were whacking noises, shouts, tears, abrupt orders, the sound of children's footsteps reluctantly ascending the stairs.

'You've ruined my anniversary,' said Maddy elegiacally, as they went by Paula's door. 'Now she's mad. And when she's mad, she stays mad.'

'I lost my ball.'

'Oh, your ball. What about my presents?'

Then their voices passed out of earshot upstairs.

Lucien and Madeleine Gauvreau lived in the larger of two apartments on the top floor of the old house. A salesman of small electric motors and switches, on the road covering his territory six days a week, Lucien was a stubby pale silent chap who trailed a dreadful hint of ill-health behind him like a puff of mist. Madeleine exhibited none of her husband's debility; she was a vivid attractive girl in her thirties, usually tanned, smartly dressed whenever she emerged from her eyrie, which was not often, with three small girls to clothe, bathe, feed, with the two eldest going to school and the third chronically a mother's girl who hung perpetually about her knees.

Madeleine and Paula weren't exactly friends; their relation was habitually distant. But Paula was Madeleine's link to the outside world, so to speak. Paula was blessedly without infant issue and could move easily about on impulse. For about eighteen months, ever since she had moved into the building, Paula had been increasingly aware of the odd ambiguity of Madeleine's feelings towards her.

Paula might possess independence of movement but she, Madeleine, had borne and begun to raise three daughters. Paula's husband (moving drowsily about between bedroom and bathroom at eleven o'clock this morning) might work at home, might treat Paula as a friend and fellow human while Lucien struggled to meet expenses, grew paler, and never got home before nine at night. But no one could say, Madeleine's manner insistently affirmed, that Paula was better married or happier.

And nevertheless there was something in her behaviour that repeatedly suggested that this indeed was precisely what she felt and resented, what she envied Paula for. The suggestion made Paula uncomfortable; there was such a marked distillate of resentment in Mrs. Gauvreau's attitude.

There were eight apartments in that old house, no two of them alike. The Gauvreaus' certainly was the most attractive although it had disadvantages as well. The enormous living-room, panelled in a superior blond walnut, had been the billiard room once upon a time and there was still a rack for cues hanging on the wall. The Gauvreaus used it ás an intolerably complex coat-closet. Kath sometimes used it for her ballet exercises. There were still four deep indentations on the excellent hardwood floor where the feet of the billiard table had left marks.

In this regularly hexagonal game-room Madeleine and the children did most of their living, playing and fighting; there was no place else in the apartment to do it for opening out of the room's six sides were a narrow railed balcony where Madeleine hung out her washing, the kitchen with the automatic washer, an enormous walk-in closet which had formerly been a gun-room, a totally inadequate bathroom always like Grand Central at six-thirty A.M., the girls' bedroom-playroom in which they flatly refused to play because the ceiling sloped and it was hot, and the small bedroom shared by Lucien and his wife. None of these rooms were connected. Everything gave onto the centre room and insensibly one's total life focused there.

Madeleine used to protest that she was drowning in blond

walnut. But Lucien loved the fine old room, with beer and the fights on TV. He was hardly ever in the room until the girls were in bed. It was a confining situation all round.

Her descent from the clouds and violent dismissal of the little girls had served as a kind of catharsis for the beleaguered Madeleine. All of a sudden everything seemed, in one of her obsessive phrases: *Just too much.* Sighting, as she swept back into the hall, the half-open door of Joe and Paula's apartment, she paused tentatively, mumbling angrily and very audibly to herself, and then burst into their hall without so much as a shouted 'Hello!' by way of warning.

It was therefore with considerable astonishment and chagrin that she was received by Joe who had been talking over his shoulder, semi-conscious, only half expecting to be heard above the rush of water in the basin, to Paula. He had gone on talking while this whirlwind sprite of a Madeleine was borne on the wings of her own tempest down the hall and into the living-room. Preoccupied with his reflection in the bathroom mirror, glumly inspecting the five cuts on his chin – he was congenitally incapable of changing razor-blades when reason and common-sense dictated – Joe had gone on muttering Sibylline morning wisdom, all the while fancying that he and Paula were alone. Picture his puzzlement when, half hearing the rumblings of discontent behind him, he turned, clad in his shorts and his inertia and nothing else, to find Madeleine, livid, developing her general dissatisfaction to his naked back.

He stared at her saucer-eyed and unembarrassed; she seemed like a truculent and hectoring ghost; she had no social focus for her fulminations, was grandly addressing the world at large and not at all his suddenly presented hairy chest.

'Hadn't I better put a shirt on?' he volunteered.

'For God's sake, Joe! I've seen a naked man before. Boy!' she continued, 'Have I ever! What a thrill!'

'It's not so much,' he admitted.

'Hairy legs and chest.'

Joe felt a twinge of irritation at this; he was certainly excessively hirsute. It was a frequent source of Paula's bouts of marriage-bed hilarity. He tickled her, it seemed. 'It keeps me warm,' he said lamely.

'Men are lucky. Lucien gets all hot and bothered by panty-girdle ads.' At this point Paula came into the room rather reluctantly. She wasn't sure whether Madeleine knew that she had been eavesdropping on the children. It hadn't been done really deliberately anyway; and all she had in fact learned was that Madeleine planned to go downtown if her blue leather gloves would stand a darning.

The children in an apartment house or real estate development are magnificently efficient transmitters of dirty linen. They operate like a radar or some such electronic device to register and communicate their parents' hatreds and disturbances. There were three speedy murders committed on Long Island just last week, the direct result of this infantine facility of communication. But Paula was not thinking specifically of murders or terrors, only desiring to smooth over and conciliate.

'Anyone for tea and cookies?' she threw out uneasily, all queasy conscience and fake neighbourliness.

'Tea!' spat Madeleine as though the harmless beverage were an obscenity. 'What about coffee?'

'What about my breakfast?' said Joe morosely.

'Coffee for three and one breakfast for the Mister.'

'You're in a very good mood,' said Madeleine with envy and Paula inferred that some days one can't do anything tactfully. She edged into the adjoining kitchen, prepared by certain signals for the impending storm. It came immediately and violently.

'You'll have to baby-sit for me this afternoon, one of you.' It was a statement of desperate fact, not a request; it was not a time, then, for polite requests.

'We'll both go up. Do you want us for all afternoon?'

'All afternoon.'

'Stop at the door when you leave.' Joe was afraid to ask where she was going – it might be only as far as downtown or it might be the final flight to Buenos Aires where she would take up with a vice-ring of international ramifications. He pleased himself with the fancy and then paid her further attention.

'I tell you,' she said, semi-hysterically, 'I will not stand for any more of this.'

Joe looked at Paula emerging from the kitchen laden with

coffee cups and jam. 'Look, Madeleine,' he said with trepidation, 'would you like me to go for a walk so you can talk to Paula?' Madeleine ignored the objection and Paula glared at him surreptitiously.

'The hell with it,' said Madeleine. 'I've got nothing to hide. You know all about me or if you don't you're the only ones in the building.'

He mumbled another apologetic phrase which she ignored.

'Another pregnancy,' she howled, launched on her career, 'another pregnancy, the doctor says and *this*' – she pointed to a lump of scar tissue on her forehead between her brows – '*this* will metastasize. And Father McCorkell says on no account to use artificial devices. And Lucien, the selfish idiot, wants a boy. I, I'm thirty-six. I've had my fill of washing diapers and going without a winter coat for the sake of the girls. It's all right I suppose, I shouldn't mind, I don't mind,' she concluded, reasoning herself into it despite her irritation. 'I like the girls to have pretty things. But we have no insurance. We need a new chair in the living-room. What am I to do? I cannot stand one more minute of this.'

She was in full flood now and not to be stopped.

'Lucien is a child, a complete child; his adolescence has lasted twenty years. We have a quarrel and I have to make it up. He never makes an overture; he never admits anything. Now it stands to reason, doesn't it, that I can't be wrong every time? I mean, it should even out, shouldn't it, over the long run? I mean, he might be wrong forty per cent of the time, giving him the best of it. But does he apologize forty per cent of the time? No! It's always me. His feet smell in bed but would I ever dare tell him that? He'd never never forget it. Once, two years ago, I hinted that I didn't want his mother over from Providence *every* holiday weekend. Can you imagine? Ever since we've been married. She hasn't missed one. There's a dirty bed in the living-room which I have to make and unmake. It turns the whole place into a sea of dirty sheets. He has brothers and sisters too but do you think she ever goes to see them? Never!

'I told Father McCorkell all this and once I got Lucien to go over to talk to him. And later on Father McCorkell told me Lucien was still an adolescent. But what good does knowing that do me? He has that damned awful job. He's never home till nine o'clock. I just finish putting the kids to bed and washing their dirty dishes and I've got to start getting his supper. I don't get the kitchen cleaned up till eleven or eleven-thirty and he has to be out of the house by seven.

'And at that he isn't making enough money,' she said.

'I'm tired of it,' she said.

She walked up and down and then sank into a chair and puddled despondently in her coffee cup. Paula thought to console her: 'You turn the girls out so beautifully. They're the best-behaved children I know.'

'Huh! They're nothing compared to Lucien. You just don't know. So I tell you what, I'm going down to the rectory today. I'm going to find out about separations, how they work. It isn't the same as a divorce. But you can get one if you've got a good reason. God knows, I'd like to have had a boy.'

Joe and Paula looked at each other uneasily, unsure what to say.

'Don't look so upset, you two,' she said, as though she had every right to disturb them with 'there but for the Grace of God' reflections. 'I'll come by around two. You won't have to do anything to Sandra. Kath is pretty good with her, thank God. She may smell a bit but you'll get used to it.' She rose, breaking her coffee cup accidentally, and left the apartment hastily. As the door slammed Joe rolled his eyes at Paula and went back to resume his interrupted bloody tussle with his whiskers.

At two o'clock they went up to look after Kath, Maddy, and Sandra. Feeling that Kath rather resented their ursurpation of her authority, Joe and Paula sat silently and moodily in a corner of the living-room engulfed in blond walnut and sombre thoughts.

'You'll be baby-sitting for us next week,' said Maddy with secure certitude.

'Why?'

'Our anniversary.'

'Their anniversary and your birthday,' said Paula, remembering the conversation on the porch.

'That's right,' said Maddy. 'I was born on their anniversary. How did you know?'

'I heard it somewhere,' said Paula vaguely. 'What do you want for your birthday?' She remembered too late that she was setting a dangerous precedent.

'I'll wait and see what I get,' said Maddy with that wonderful assurance. 'I'll tell you then. Mummy's gone downtown today to look at presents. I think,' she concluded, 'I think she's planning to surprise me.'

High Fidelity

MRS. GARVEY had made up a little white card, copying it from the calendar, a square for every business day; there was space on the card for about forty-five weekdays, that is, about two months' work. She liked to have one customer in view for each square – two months' work lined up in advance – and she had her schedule so arranged that she visited each customer in rotation. By the time she made a second visit, her customers' apartments were always ready for a thorough cleaning. In two months on the upper East Side windowsills become pretty gritty, the floors under the beds are festooned with enormous dustballs. Everything needs vacuuming and polishing. She liked to have her card full, each square an appointment, with the time and her means of gaining entrance to the apartment noted in the square. Most of her customers were young working couples and they often forgot to leave a key.

She also kept a little book with the names and telephone numbers of her customers listed under three headings: Old Customers, New Customers, Prospects. She hated to see the number listed go below forty-five and was always asking her employers, on the telephone or at their rare personal meetings, to recommend her to their friends.

She ran her little business systematically, as can be seen, usually worked from one till five, leaving the apartment spick and span just before her employers came home. She liked to keep it that way, sort of impersonal, because she couldn't cope with the domestic problems of forty-five customers. They paid her eight dollars for the four hours, leaving it on the kitchen table with a couple of subway tokens, and with any special instructions in writing. She worked five days a week, made forty dollars, paid her income tax punctiliously, and got along just fine. She was able to send carefully chosen birthday presents every year to her six grandchildren who lived in the Bronx, and in New Rochelle. Her mornings were her own to drum up new business or to do with as she pleased. She led an even, disciplined, comfortable life, as long as she could count forty-five customers in her book. When the number sank much below that, she worried.

Coming along 87th Street this afternoon, she felt particularly pleased with herself at opening up a new account because it brought the number up to forty-nine, giving her a bit of a cushion. Business had been holding fairly steady through the last six months or so. She was not an investor, but if she had been a reader of the financial columns she would have been interested to discover that a graph representing the number of her customers would have described very accurately the fluctuations in the economy. When stock prices fall, young couples clean their own apartments.

She was pleased to see that the building in which young Mr. and Mrs. Sansone lived was provided with a doorman who smiled at her as she paused in the doorway.

'Six-F?' he said.

'That's right.'

'They left it with me,' he said, handing her a key. 'You can't be too careful, even in this neighbourhood.' He began to describe two cases of breaking and entering that had occurred in the building. No one understood how the thieves had gotten past the front door. *He* had been right there the whole time and could prove it. *Had* proved it when the agent had interrogated him.

Mrs. Garvey tried to edge away towards the elevator without being obviously rude. Sometimes these doormen were of considerable help to her when a customer forgot to leave a key, so she tried to maintain good relations with them. But she didn't want to be late. She felt that as she was being paid for four hours' work she ought to be inside the apartment for the whole time. And she liked to leave sharp at five. She had to sidle backwards into the elevator, smiling at the doorman and seeming to listen politely to his apology for his conduct.

Going up in the elevator she consulted a little Bulova watch which was pinned to her bodice like a brooch. Her son Thomas had given it to her, Christmas before last, and it kept very good time. She was glad to see that it lacked five minutes of the hour. She got out of the elevator and started down the hall.

All the way down, she heard the trains, getting louder and

nearer. At first she thought that she was imagining it but as she drew closer to Six-f she knew that she really heard them. Trains. Very loud, shunting and whistling and puffing, bells ringing, and once, even, a brakeman's shout of warning. Then there came the sound of boxcars colliding heavily, and an unmistakable loud ding-dong, and all these sounds repeated themselves over and over. It was as though there were a roundhouse just inside the door. As she opened it, she half expected to see a brakeman waving a lantern at her to get out of the way. In the diminutive hall the sound was deafening but not alarming because she knew by now what it really was.

She went inside the living-room and stared at the phonograph, wondering if Mrs. Sansone had left it on for some particular reason. She had seen things like these many times before; almost all her customers owned them, some enormous, some conveniently small. She felt more at home with those in wooden cabinets because they were like radios, easy to dust, whereas the others had tubes sticking out of them – she knew what a tube was, having owned a radio for over thirty years – and these tubes were fragile and hard to dust behind. They could be damaged, she knew, or even broken, very easily.

The Sansones' phonograph had tubes sticking out on top. There was a turntable on which a disc was spinning and spinning; the disc had a very deep gouge in it – she knew that a gouge was not good for them – and was simply repeating itself over and over. Then there was a metal box like a short-wave set, with the tubes and a little red light, and on this box were many dials, above one of which was printed VOLUME, ON-OFF. There was also a sound-box or loudspeaker across the room, from which the sound of the trains came.

She felt the thing like a short-wave set with a tentative innocent hand, and found it very hot to the touch. She was nearly certain that the machine shouldn't be on – that it had been left on by mistake, though how that could be she didn't understand, so she twisted the ON-OFF dial until the red light went out and the sound stopped. She looked carefully at the record on the turntable; surely it had been damaged, whether accidentally or not she couldn't tell. But the scratch – it was really much more than a scratch – must have been produced by some considerable shock, like a sharp push or a blow. She made a mental note to dust with caution in that part of the living-room; there didn't seem to be very many records around but she wanted to be quite sure that she didn't step on one, or knock one down.

Her money and transportation lay on the kitchen table; there were no special written instructions, so she set to work in her usual efficient style.

It was a very small apartment, a tiny living-room, a tinier bedroom hardly big enough to take the enormous double bed, a kitchen-cubicle, bath and closets. Even a working wife, she thought to herself, should be able to keep up a place like this, doing a little bit every night. But perhaps Mrs. Sansone was allergic to dust or something.

The phonograph was just a little one, a beginner's set; she could tell by comparing it with those she'd seen elsewhere. But it dominated the room simply because the room was so very small. And the bedroom was much smaller still, so small that she could scarcely get the vacuum in the door and the hose under the enormous unmade bed, to go after the dustballs. It wasn't part of her customary assignment to make beds – she wasn't a chambermaid, after all – but she did so, this once, as a courtesy to a new customer, meaning not to do it again.

By about three-thirty she had the worst of the mess cleaned up, the sheets changed, the blankets pulled drum-tight on the aired and fresh-smelling bed, the closets aired, sprayed, de-mothed, vacuumed, the floors waxed and polished. She could tell that Mrs. Sansone's electric polisher had never been used. The rotary pads were brand new.

After she had the worst of the mess straightened around, she began to add those virtuoso finishing touches that kept her services so much in demand, scrubbing the sinks and basins, even the toilet-bowl, dusting in places where no one normally dusts. And here she made a slight slip which bothered her considerably. As she was dusting behind the phonograph, she caught hold of one of the little tubes, or rather, it caught in her sleeve, and the rubbing motion of her arm popped it out of its socket; it must have been inserted improperly. Anyway it rolled away from her clutch and fell about six inches, bouncing on the shelf which held the phonograph.

She knew nothing whatsoever about these machines, and wondered what to do with the little tube. She might simply have shoved it back into place but concealment was foreign to her nature. She carefully traced the electric cord back to the wall plug, disconnecting the phonograph before she experimented, and then attempted to insert the tube properly, first rubbing the dirty glass till it shone. But she found it hard to push the little thing into place, and wasn't sure that she had managed it correctly.

By now it was getting on towards five o'clock. She hunted up a pencil and paper and wrote a careful account of what she had done with the tube, leaving the note in the kitchen where she had found her money. She mentioned the date of her next call and asked Mrs. Sansone to call and confirm. She said that she was sorry about the tube and hoped it wasn't broken but if it was, the Sansones could deduct the cost from her next payment. Then she cleaned herself and left the apartment a little bit after five, her conscience bothered just the least bit about that little tube. As she walked towards the Second Avenue bus stop, she saw a distracted young girl, dark and pretty, pass her on the other side of the street. She had an idea that it might be her afternoon's employer, but didn't speak to her.

The following week she got a confirmatory call from the Sansones; nothing was said about the phonograph.

She was happy to go back to the tiny apartment because it suited her schedule so well. She tried to arrange her work so that she did a couple of big places each week, and a couple of smaller ones, so that she didn't have to work equally hard every day. The Sansone place was so small that it was practically a holiday for her; four hours was twice as much time as an experienced cleaning woman needed for the job. She sometimes asked herself if she shouldn't perhaps make a special rate for those with small apartments and then decided, very reasonably, that she was being paid, not by the hour, but by the call, like a doctor. If she cut her rate, she would have to make two calls in an afternoon, and she couldn't do it in the allotted time. She decided that she could always find a few little extra things to do, to make it worth the full eight dollars.

She needn't have worried. When she came for the second

time into little Apartment Six-f, she saw that there would be plenty to do. Not only had the place reverted to its former jungle state, probably immediately after her last visit; it was in worse shape than before, dirtier and more disarranged. Mrs. Sansone could hardly be doing anything at all in the line of housework; perhaps she didn't like it very much, or wasn't used to it. There were a few changes in the arrangement of the place – small twin beds in the bedroom, instead of the enormous double, which made the room much easier to clean – but nothing that made a great deal of difference to Mrs. Garvey.

Nothing very much. There *was* one quite striking and immediately obvious change. Where before there had been the beginner's phonograph and very few records, now there was a big cabinet model and hundreds and hundreds of records, lying all over the living-room. She looked at some of their titles and they seemed nonsensical to her: bird calls, locomotive noises, brass bands, feet on a subway grating, fire trucks, Burmese folk songs, and somebody called David Tudor, whose picture was on the cover of one record and who looked like a fine young man, dark and handsome, though nervous. She saw no records of music but supposed that there must be some.

She wondered what to do with the records; they were all over the floor and would have to be moved if she was to do anything with the living-room. She wondered idly to whom they belonged. Picking one up very carefully, noting the exact place on the dusty carpet where it had lain, she examined it closely, turning it over and over. On the back, at the top, was written in a tight clear hand: BASS MINUS TWO, TREBLE PLUS TWO, AES CURVE, CUTOUT FF6000-8000. She carried the record carefully into the kitchen and compared it with a short note which Mrs. Sansone had left. They were different.

All the note from Mrs. Sansone said was: 'You needn't worry about that stupid tube.' Her eight dollars was all there.

She had an idea that record collectors kept their disks in some sort of order but since there seemed to be no way of telling what it might be in this case she simply picked them all up and slipped them into the different record racks which stood here and there. The record racks were horribly dusty and she decided to go over them carefully if she had time.

But she didn't have time; she collected two full vacuum bags of dust doing the basic cleaning – the groundwork – and only had time to take a cursory swipe at the record racks. When she saw that she was raising a lot of new dust she let them go with a lick and a promise, meaning to have another go at them on her next visit, if she had time, which didn't seem likely.

As she left the building, the doorman, the same one as before, eyed her speculatively, as though he'd like to question her if it weren't for her manner which was calculated to discourage any discussion of her employers. She asked no questions and answered none.

Stocks continued high and her appointment card showed it; she went busily and happily from apartment to apartment, never thinking of anything connected with her work except the rooms she happened to be cleaning at the time. A less equable person might have collected much to upset her and even render her temperament somewhat cheerless. But like all the innocent, Mrs. Garvey came and went in the midst of fire and flood, unscathed by it all, her world circumscribed by the First and Second Avenue buses, with the Bronx and New Rochelle as distant gardens of blissful ease.

Some of her customers had a blanket arrangement with her whereby she simply scheduled her visits as much as six months, and in one case a year, in advance. But mostly they went along from one call to the next and she preferred it that way because, while she liked to keep personal contact to a minimum – she had learned that it was better that way – she wanted to be sure that her customers were still alive and thinking of her now and then.

Two years ago she had had a rotten fright from one bachelor. He had retained her on a six-month basis, paying her in advance, which she wasn't too happy about. When she got money in advance, she would go out and buy a birthday present or a length of yard goods for her daughter or daughter-in-law, and then she would be short a day's pay later on. Anyway she went up to this bachelor's apartment one day without having spoken to him in six months; she found him dead in bed, quite a young man too. Her name had been in the papers, which she didn't like. It had been only a short paragraph because there had been nothing sensational or suspicious about his death – it had been his heart – but there it was, it didn't look right. Her customers wouldn't like it. So she liked to talk to them on the phone occasionally, just to make sure.

Mrs. Sansone didn't call her back until two months were almost up and when she did, she sounded dubious, as though she weren't sure she needed a cleaning woman. If anyone did, she did.

'I guess we'll try it once more,' she said indecisively, rather offending poor Mrs. Garvey.

'I'll be there,' said Mrs. Garvey brightly, trying to encourage her, 'and I'll get after those record racks this time. You won't recognize them when I'm finished.'

Mrs. Sansone muttered something inarticulate and then her voice grew louder. 'I'm afraid they're an awful nuisance,' she said.

'Oh, no,' said Mrs. Garvey, 'they just need careful looking after. I'll be there on Thursday as usual.'

But on Thursday she was late and had to hurry to make her appointment; she had spent the morning with her Bronx grandchildren because Betty had gone downtown to have an early lunch with Thomas, a thing she did quite often which Mrs. Garvey thoroughly approved of, as she did everything about her daughter-in-law. There was nothing of the conventional mother-in-law about Mrs. Garvey. She loved Betty and regarded her as her own daughter.

The morning with the three steamrollers, as she called them, had left her a bit worn. She planned to have a cup of instant coffee about three o'clock, to break up the afternoon and give her a chance to catch her breath. She puffed along 87th Street and grabbed the key from the doorman on the dead run, hardly stopping to nod to him, and even shaking him off without listening to what he had to say; the man was a bit of a gossip.

When she was inside the apartment, in the tiny hall, she stopped and looked at her watch, twenty past one. That meant she'd be twenty minutes late getting out. She leaned against the door puffing and trying to catch her breath. She was getting too old to play horsie with the steamrollers all morning and then come straight on to work. She decided to take a few minutes' rest before she got started.

In the living-room she collapsed in the only big armchair and closed her eyes, without looking about her. She was really quite tired and she let her head fall back against the chair for a few moments. Then she slowly began to be aware of a faint but unmistakable alteration in the mood, the tone, the atmosphere, of the apartment. She tried, without looking up, to make out what it was and soon realized that there was a low but powerful humming noise all around her, so faint that she could just make it out. She didn't see how it could be the phonograph because it was all around her instead of just in the corner; but it sounded as if they'd forgotten and left it on again. She opened her eyes reluctantly, stood up, and looked around the room.

The cabinet phonograph which she'd seen last time was no longer there. Instead, in diagonally opposite corners of the room, like fantastic corner cupboards, were two gigantic loud-speakers humming quietly to themselves, filling the apartment with the sound. Stereophonic sound, she realized. She had never heard it before but had seen it advertised.

Right beside one of the speakers, the sofa was folded out as a bed; she had never realized that it was a convertible. And hanging in the speaker next to the bed, right in the middle of the fabric which shielded the horn, was a woman's shoe, suspended by its spike heel. There was a big rent in the fabric.

She crossed to the broken speaker and gently pulled the shoe out, disentangling it with some difficulty. She examined the horn behind the fabric. It was dented and there seemed to be a break in it.

She went into the bedroom holding the shoe in her hand and there she found its mate, kicked halfway under one of the twin beds, the one which was still neatly made up. She hung both shoes in their proper place in the bag in Mrs. Sansone's closet.

She didn't enjoy her afternoon's work, even the coffee which she allowed herself at three, but she did just as good a job as she always did, leaving at twenty minutes past five.

That night she went through her list of 'Prospects' carefully. For some obscure reason, she thought that the Sansones might not invite her back. And when two months had gone by and their time came round again, she understood sorrowfully that she was right. She never heard of them again.

The Regulars

ALL THE MEN in the neighbourhood go to Dante D'Imonte's place on Friday and Saturday nights, treating it as a kind of clubhouse, and meeting their friends there as a matter of course. Nobody brings his wife, not to the bar. Sometimes one of the regulars will take his wife out to dinner through the week, to give her a treat, if they have kids old enough to look after the babies. They don't approve of baby-sitters, these people. Baby-sitters are for clerks and executives. Dante's customers would feel queer about leaving their youngest children in the care of a stranger, even a neighbourhood girl.

You can get a pretty good dinner there including shrimp cocktail and a club steak for two-fifty, plus tip, and you needn't leave a big tip. The three waitresses, Roselee, Gail, and Bernarda, live in the neighbourhood and would be offended if anybody tried to treat them like servants or something. Thirty-five cents is enough on the two-fifty dinner, maybe an eighty-cent tip for a man and his wife.

Dante calls his place Delmonico's and he tries to carry on the tradition of fine food and good fellowship. He isn't running a pizzeria, you understand, but a real restaurant. It isn't a bar-and-grill type of place either; there are no pinball machines. On the south side of the building is the dining-room, with the parking lot behind it, and to the north, the men's bar, where you can have a sandwich brought to you if you want.

You aren't encouraged to eat in the men's bar. If you want to eat, you should go to the dining-room and sit down properly with a tablecloth and a waitress to look after you. If he knows you, and he will if you live anywhere in the neighbourhood, Dante comes over and says hello, telling you what's good tonight. He won't sit down.

After the dinner hour on Friday and Saturday nights, he goes into the men's bar to circulate, talking to everybody, trying to make them feel good, making sure a man doesn't have to wait too long between beers. He hates to see an empty glass stand in front of a man for too long. But he doesn't push you to empty your glass; he just likes to see something in it. Drunkenness is not encouraged in Delmonico's and a man who can't hold it, or who gets nasty, can't make it as one of the regulars. He just isn't made welcome and soon he gets the idea. There have been one or two exceptions made, like poor old Bodza Mulhearne, but that's absolutely all.

The men's bar has a row of eighteen stools. Along the north wall are six small tables for two, and in the back of the room are eight more tables, seating four. These sixty-two spaces are nearly always filled to capacity on the weekend, from eight-thirty until closing. That doesn't mean that there are only sixty-two regulars and that nobody else can come in. There are probably a hundred to a hundred and twenty regulars, maybe more. Dante has tried to figure it out from time to time, making a pencil list on an old menu card, to see how much trade he can count on. Say a hundred and twenty-five, which sounds about right.

But they don't all come in both nights and they don't stay all night. Some come in right after dinner and have a couple of beers before the bowling up the street. Some come, or used to come, just from ten to eleven on Friday to watch the TV fight. There are a few who close the place on Friday and they usually don't come in at all on Saturday. So it goes.

There are twenty to twenty-five of us who come in on both Friday and Saturday nights all the year round except during holiday time in the summer. We all know each other. Most of the guys have seen each other almost every day since they were kids going to Saint Clare's or to Whitney Public. The oldest of this hard core are in their early fifties; in the late fifties they stop coming to stay at home with the grandchildren while the younger men begin to come. The youngest are the young married guys around twenty-five. You get a good cross-section of neighbourhood opinion listening to the talk, except where politics are concerned. Everybody's a Democrat.

In 1952 Pete Scavo voted for Eisenhower because he was a good leader and a war hero and all that, and somebody found out about it. Now everybody calls him 'Banker Pete'. He hasn't felt the same since. He's an electrician with his own shop and a helper, which puts him in the employer class, not like the rest of us. Old Banker Pete! He's a pretty good guy.

Most of the guys work for the Electric or the Aircraft. When they struck the Aircraft in the spring, Dante nearly died he was so upset. He did about the same amount of business but a lot of it was on the tab, which he doesn't like at all. He had to run tabs though, or he'd have lost all his regulars.

'The guys gotta have their beer,' he would say, pulling a long face, 'strike or no strike.'

Then all at once the strike was over and the overtime began to pick up. The patrons kept coming in to pay off their tabs and he was happy again. He'd be standing at the register, making change for twenties, smiling and gabbing away. He didn't have to write off a single account. It pays to get to know your trade and Dante knows this. He studies the situation.

Like with Bodza Mulhearne, the night the fights went off the air for good. When they come back in the fall it won't be the same at all because they're going to be broadcast on Saturday night which is no good. You're not free the next day. Sunday A.M. most of the regulars have to get up and go to church, so they don't really relax, load up, and enjoy themselves the way they used to on Friday night.

The correct night for the TV fights was Friday and way back just after the war, when they first came on the air, the sponsors made the right choice of a day. It was sort of an institution at Delmonico's, the Friday night fights, for twelve or thirteen years, and now they're gone for good. Well, that's the way.

Everybody was sitting around waiting for the last fight to come on and feeling sort of sad, you know. For most of the men under forty, there had always been Friday night fights; most of them were too young to come during or after the war so their earliest memories of the place are all mixed up with the fights – Jakie LaMotta, Sugar Ray, Billy Graham, Chico Vejar, Ike Williams, Chuck Davey, Archie Moore, Bob Satterfield, Kid Gavilan – all the famous fighters from the late forties and early fifties.

Even the older men felt it because when television first came on they had been in their thirties and now they're nearly ready to stay at home with the grandchildren. It was sad. That's a long time you know, thirteen years. Long enough for a kid to grow up or a man to grow old.

Along about nine, nine-thirty, a few of us began to put it

away a little faster than usual – kind of a celebration, or perhaps a wake. That's it. It was more like a wake because everybody was going to miss the fights, and Dante most of all.

You get something good going on the TV and right away they take it off. The working man has no choice in it. They just take it off without giving you any chance to express an opinion. So the guys were drinking a little more than usual, nothing riotous, and talking it up, down at the end of the bar by the register.

At nine-thirty a stranger came in, a young lad about twenty-four or five, a nice-looking kid, probably a Guinea like the rest of them. He was carrying a book and he stood in the doorway sort of nervously, as though he wasn't sure he had a right to come in. The fact is, it isn't everybody who's welcome at Dante's place. He doesn't like rummies and won't let them in; he sends them over to Saint Clare's Rectory to see Father Colton; they cause trouble with the police and the welfare. He also doesn't like one-beer drinkers who'll take up a stool for three hours, spending fifteen cents the whole time.

Most of all he doesn't like the upper-class people who drop in now and then. A lot of them live two blocks over by the river, in expensive apartments, and sometimes they come into Delmonico's and make a lot of smart remarks about how quaint it is, and about the wonderful primitive types who go there. They aren't welcome. But this fellow didn't look like a rummy or a deadbeat or a playboy, but like a nice quiet boy who was probably somebody's cousin in the neighbourhood. He sat down at the bar, on a stool by the door away from the regulars, and Sal went over to see what he wanted.

'Bottle of Lowenbrau,' he said. Everybody snickered when they heard this.

'Cost you sixty-five cents,' said Sal.

'All right,' he said, smiling nicely at Sal.

When Sal set the bottle and glass in front of him, he handed Sal a dollar.

'I can run your check for you, if you're going to be here a while.' Most new people want to run a check and Sal usually checks with Dante. It's a little favour that you don't do for everybody. Sal looked down the bar at Dante and he nodded; the kid looked fine to him.

'I don't know how long I'll stay,' he said. Sal handed him his change and he said, 'Keep it.' You couldn't tell whether Sal was pleased or not. He doesn't like to take money from just anybody who wanders in. I know that sounds funny but it's true.

'Why, thanks,' he said, 'can I get you anything else?'

'Yes, you can. You could ask the dining room if I could have a shrimp cocktail in here.' He was polite and nice and everything, but he didn't waste any words. Sal looked at him for a while and then went and placed the order, shrimp cocktail and Lowenbrau! Nobody ever heard of that before. When Roselee brought it from the kitchen he paid her, tipped her – he certainly wasn't looking for trouble – and ate the shrimps. He didn't eat the lettuce.

Then he drank some of his beer and opened his book and started to read as though he was alone. Nobody could figure him out. Why would somebody go to a bar to read? Every once in a while he laughed to himself and since nobody knew what he was laughing at, it was sort of bothersome. Dante watched him closely for ten minutes and then seemed to be satisfied that he wasn't some kind of troublemaker. He might have been an inspector, don't you see, checking on whether they served minors. There's never anybody under twenty-one in Delmonico's. None of the neighbourhood kids would try it and the last time a couple of delinquents came in Dante and Sal gave them a kick in the pants and sent them on their way quick. But this lad was okay, you could see.

He finished his beer, looked up from his book and asked for another. This time he didn't give Sal the thirty-five cents.

The fight came on as usual at ten o'clock and, my God, what a pair of bums they had, to finish off the program. Thirteen years they've been on the air, and that's the best they can do! Two real canvasbacks that nobody ever heard of, Doug Jones and Von Clay, light-heavyweights. They couldn't do anything but lean on each other and waltz. After thirteen years, I guess they were scraping the bottom of the barrel.

Soon the regulars began to get on the fighters, especially Bodza Mulhearne. He's a Harp cab-driver who lives up the street. He isn't one of the regulars, strictly speaking, because he doesn't work at the Aircraft or the Electric, and he doesn't make

as much money as most of the guys. To hear Bodza tell it, he's
been present at every important sports event since before he was
born. He comes in every Friday and Saturday night, and Dante
speaks to him, but you couldn't call him a real regular, more on
the fringe.

He always squeezes in between two or three of the regulars
and acts like he belongs, and in a way he does. At least Dante
hasn't shooed him out, and he's been coming for years. Well, he
didn't like the fight. He thought it was a lousy fight to finish up
the season with. He started to say so in the first round and he
kept it up. Every time Jimmy Powers would say something on
the TV, Bodza would be right there with some smarter answer.

'Clay's a good hooker, with power in both hands,' said
Jimmy Powers.

'What do you know, Powers, what do you know?' Bodza
shouted. He kept trying to get the other guys to shout along
with him, slapping them on the back and telling them what a
bad fight it was. But mostly they just sat and looked at the screen
and were quiet. It made Bodza mad, and of course he had had
more beer than usual; we all had. Finally he began to make
remarks about the strange kid at the other end of the bar. At first
he was quiet and then he got noisier. He isn't a bad little guy; it's
just that he wants to be noticed.

'Lowenbrau,' he kept mumbling, 'Lowenbrau, for Christ's
sake. What's the matter with Knick, will somebody tell me?'

Banker Pete and some of the other guys warned him to be
quiet, and Dante was eyeing him, but he wouldn't shut up.

'Jeez,' he kept saying, 'jeez, my evening's ruined. First the
Lowenbrau kid, and now this stinking fight. Hey, kid,' he said,
quietly at first because he was afraid of Dante, then louder when
he noticed that Dante didn't say anything to him, 'hey, kid,
what's your name?'

The strange kid went on reading, probably didn't even realize that Bodza was talking to him; the noise of the TV made all
the voices in the room blend. Sometimes he put his book down
for a second and looked at the TV, and somehow you got the
impression that he knew something about boxing. He nodded
his head in the right places. Then he would go back to his book.
When he looked at the screen he would order another beer,

giving Sal the change on every second round. He could put it away pretty good in a quiet way, giving no offence. For a long time Bodza couldn't get any reaction out of him.

It made him mad to be ignored like that, so he turned to Dante, who was sitting at a table in the back, and began to ask him about the kid in a loud insulting voice.

'What's the matter, Dante,' he said, 'you letting everybody come in here? Who is this guy, anyway? He looks under twenty-one to me. Why don't you ask him, Dante?'

Dante didn't pay much attention. He didn't like the way Bodza was going on, you could see, but he was an old customer and never caused any trouble before, so Dante watched and went along with him. He'd smile at Bodza, and watch to see that he didn't get too rough. There was nothing to it actually; it was just that everybody felt low.

'How old are you, kid? What's your name, eh? What's your name?' He began to mimic the stranger. 'Can I have a shrimp cocktail, please, mummy? Jesus Christ,' he would say, 'Jesus Christ!'

By now the noise on the TV was getting pretty loud and everybody was talking it up, not just about the fight, but different things, the Japanese situation, taxes, the Democratic nomination, the bowling, and it was much too noisy to read, so the boy closed his book and looked around as though he'd been asleep. He smiled at nothing, emptied his glass, and ordered another, politely and quietly. Sal spoke to him when he brought the beer.

'You live around here?'

'Yes,' he said.

Bodza broke in. 'Where do you live, hey? What's your address, sonny? Let me see your driver's licence.'

All at once the boy caught on, for the first time. He looked at Bodza, who was ten or twelve stools away from him, down the bar in the middle of the crowd, and not afraid of anything because he had the regulars all around him.

'Yes, it's you I'm talking to,' said Bodza, pretty loud. 'Where do you come from?' The kid smiled uncertainly.

'Where do you get that stuff with the Lowenbrau? Isn't American beer good enough for you? Maybe you're a German

or something, hey?' He was really pretty ugly about it. Banker
Pete and Gus Lamantia and one or two others were trying to get
him to sit with them at a table in the back but he wouldn't let
himself be distracted; you know how they are. He wasn't used
to drinking that much in one night.

'Where's his cab?' said Gus to Dante under his breath. 'We'd
better not let him drive it home.' Bodza heard this.

'Oh,' he said, very hurt, 'that's my pal Gus! Going to take his
side, are you? Think I'm drunk, do you? Well, you're wrong,
buddy.' He got off his stool and started to move up the bar, not
walking very well. Just then the fights went off the air and there
was a shout ... almost more of ... well, a wail ... from the crowd.
They were going to miss the fights.

'They're gone,' said Bodza, very upset, 'gone for good.' He
was all set to blame it on the kid.

'What do you know about fights?' said Bodza. 'You think
Von Clay is a fighter?'

The kid picked up his book and looked around for Sal.

'That's right,' said Bodza, 'you'd better get out of here.
You're not wanted.' Everybody began to tire of the whole business.

'Knock it off, Bodza,' they said.

'Leave the kid alone.'

He began to feel that he wasn't being supported so he turned
and staggered down the passageway towards the dining-room.
The kid paid his check and started out the door.

'Hey, kid. Hey, fellow,' Gus Lamantia called to him. He
turned around. 'Listen,' said Gus, 'no hard feelings, eh? We've
got a nice bunch of guys here, we really have. Come back again
sometime and don't mind Bodza. He didn't mean any harm.
He's a little drunk, that's all.'

The boy didn't say a word, just stood there looking at Gus.

'Come in again soon,' said Gus. The kid turned and went out
and in a minute Bodza came back carrying an egg sandwich. He
shouldered his way back to the bar, looking mighty big, and
some of the guys made way for him.

They weren't disgusted with Bodza because they knew how
he felt. Gus Lamantia drove his cab home for him. And since he
chased somebody out of Dante's place he's got a reputation. In a
way he's more of a regular than ever before.

From the Fields of Sleep

SO THEY CAME on a white day, thought Johnson, shifting the weight of the ammunition belt from forearm to forearm, white sand, white ocean, white sky. The shattering white light and the noise of the covering barrage blended idiotically with his terror in the morning of the final assault. A mile and a half offshore the transports were still putting over landing craft, though by now the first and second waves were nearly ashore. At a mile they resembled square black water beetles, at a thousand yards Johnson could make out arms and legs, helmets and rifles, silhouetted blankly against the glare, and Lordy there must be a million of the little black bugs, at five hundred yards they grow into human enemies coming in, in, here they ... onto the beach, up, running now and *into* the enfilading fire from the machine-gun emplacements, the belt jerking wildly in his hands as he feeds it up. Don't watch, don't look, number two man keep your head down, look what you're doing, *Keep your head down Johnson. Do you want to jam us?* What'll I do if they get up here? *Johnson!!*

The first two waves were gone a hundred per cent, we got them all − all but a couple lying kicking on the beach. OK. *Depress your angle. Don't stick it in the sand, number one man* and let's see what we can do with the ones lying in the water, see if we can get them, they'll come back to haunt us if we don't. Third wave, the big one, there's too many of them this time, what'll I do if they get up here? I have nothing to fight with only this machine gun and that's no good, where can I go? Anyway the barrage stopped and I can think. They haven't crossed the beach yet. *New belt Johnson. Get it up here.* I hope this one doesn't jam, pull it back easy now, and go! Go! If they get into the brush we're done. We can't get off the island; we can't re-form, we can't fight inland, there isn't any inland. What'll we do if they get on to stay? They'll kill us all.

There are eleven hundred men on the island counting everybody, marines, naval and air personnel, the hospital staff, the weatherman and his helpers, and the scientists, and if it weren't for the scientists we wouldn't be in this mess, they'd have bypassed us and hit something worth hitting. There's fifteen hundred miles of ocean between here and the base, and they'd have gone on and hit the base and come back for us later, without so many men. There must be a whole division coming in, a division and support troops, that's twelve thousand of them. Twelve thousand! And the only ones they'll bother to leave alive will be the scientists; they'll want to talk to them, but they don't want to talk to me. A division. We haven't got a chance. I wonder if everybody knows it, I wonder if Sergeant Brennan knows it? Look at him up there with his sunburn, we're all getting burned, it's this damned white glare, worse than sunshine. I wish the sun would come out. Look at them come. Oh, God, they're into the brush!

Why is everything so quiet all of a sudden?

Where are those bastards that went into the brush, where did they get to? What'll we do if anything happens to Brennan, who'll look after us? *Look after us,* what am I, a child or something? I hope Brennan is alive when it's over, maybe he can talk them into taking prisoners. I wish I was a prisoner somewhere right now, instead of sitting here. Somebody's going to get killed.

Where are those guys in the brush? Never mind the beach, get the ones in front, if they get to the dunes the gun will be useless, we'll be firing into sand when they rush us. I haven't even got a bayonet. Will we just go on firing until they climb in on top of us, or will they let us get out of here and go back? They won't let us do that, I know they won't. I'll go anyway. I'll run back and get behind the lines and I won't take this bloody gun with me either. There they *are, through the brush and coming at us.*

Traverse, traverse, get it around, all right number one man, hold it, hold it open fire. How can Brennan be so quiet, they can't be more than a hundred yards away. Who's going to repel them, who's going to go out and push them back? If they get to us the whole island is gone, there's nothing to stop them except the guys along the creek and they'll go through them like nothing. I wonder if they got any tanks ashore yet. Tanks'll clear the guys out of the creek and then they'll have everything, there isn't any place.

Where's the enfilading fire? Number six emplacement silenced, Sergeant, we can't establish crossfire. That's it, that is it. Now they can just walk over here and take us, and I guess that's what they're going to do. Twenty feet and flop, twenty feet and flop, we're getting some of them but not all, twenty feet and flop, in a minute they'll rush us. Those are grenades, that noise, look at them all, black. Like baseballs, look at them spin.

Now the assault wave stands up for what is plainly meant to be the last time, bayonets fixed and at the ready, and starts coming for the machine guns, running but they almost seem to be walking, as the men in emplacement number seven keep firing as the attackers walk up into them until in the last seconds they get up themselves to back away like bewildered cattle in a little huddle from the smoking gun that's failed them, that hasn't kept the attackers off after all. Johnson jiggles his helmet square on his head, reaches behind him for his rifle, stands and looks. He can see the individual members of the advancing line, count them, one two three four dozens coming into our pit.

I can see their faces, look at those bayonets, conventional weapons, Jesus! He stares fascinated by the bayonets, dull, not glittering, in the seamless white glare. That guy's looking at me. Oh, God, he's coming for *me. Going to try and get me with that thing.* He shifts his feet irresolutely on the sand in the pit, ready to run in the next instant, looks at the man running towards him, a short man with a square face, if I could talk to him, squinting, he's got drops of sweat on his face, oh, oh, he's looking at me, what'll I do, will it hurt? He's lifting his arms, *fifteen feet.*

At this instant a grenade thrown from a wide angle bursts between them, killing Johnson's attacker and dropping Johnson into unconsciousness.

When he awoke the sun was an enormous white disc in the central vault of the sky, still hidden behind the overcast but threatening at every second to break through. It was intensely hot and deathly still, the firing over, the island fallen. Now and then a burst of firing broke the stillness; cries followed each burst but these noises were only a kind of punctuation in the stillness.

He couldn't see the sun, wasn't sure that he could see at all, his head was so full of pain, a headache the like of which he'd never had before. Concussion, he thought, concussion from the blast. It had hit him like a flat piece of timber swung at his head, the impact solidly material, and his head pulsed painfully, his scalp loose and crawling as if there were insects under it. He was afraid to open his eyes because he wasn't sure that he could still see. Something heavy and limp pressed down upon him, on his face and chest and legs. As he recovered more and more of his consciousness he realized that he was nearly buried under a body, or bodies, corpses, he thought with a shudder although they hadn't yet begun to smell, corpses and sand, sand in his mouth and nose, in his hair, sand between his face and the weight on top of him.

He could move an arm, so he ran his fingers over the body closest to him, smotheringly on top of him. Almost at once he felt the rough cloth of a sleeve. He knew whose it must be before he found the stripes, Brennan, and he was right. He found the threaded tracing of the sergeant's stripes with his anxious fingers, thanking God for Brennan in a way he never had before. The brief movement nearly exhausted him and he dug his hand back into the sand, hoping that it looked as limply dead as the sergeant's body felt. His head hurt him and he couldn't think straight. Listening confusedly in the stillness he could hear gulls shrilling and crying and the movement of water on the beach, it was so still, and sometimes the brief rattle of gunfire. All at once he realized what it meant.

Dispatching the wounded, he realized with horror. They're going around firing into piles of dead and dying, but I'm not dying. He was alive and he nearly cried out with the realization, and then with horror and amazement stifled the tentative cry. Voices moved closer, gulls, waves, voices, he heard them talking and then the bursts, probably from a sub-machine gun of some type. They'll come over here and rake the emplacement. If I shout, try to stand up and tell them I'm alive, they'll simply shoot me. Which would be better, to wait for it here or to stand up? Voices moved very close now. They must be looking into emplacement number six. The sub-machine gun rattled and there was a shriek and then silence, and then Johnson's decision was taken for him, the voices came very very close and he heard a calm quiet exchange of words and smelled tobacco smoke. Two men, probably a platoon commander and his sergeant, just going along quietly policing up their area, getting rid of the dying, their own, he suspected, as well as their enemies. The voices chatted quietly while he lay below them nearly out of his mind with tension. Then the officer raked the emplacement with three long bursts and Sergeant Brennan's body leaped like a hooked fish, flopping under the impact of the bullets, and *slam* something like a hammer took Johnson in the shoulder and he bit through his lower lip not with pain but with the effort to play dead. He'd been hit in the shoulder and he had to be quiet about it. It didn't hurt. Yet!

Apparently satisfied, the officer moved away and went on with his housecleaning and Johnson lay in the sand stiff with terror and shock, beginning to feel his left shoulder sting and quiver and go warm with blood – he prayed that the flow of blood didn't show from above and he listened for the officer but heard no footsteps on the sand, and then he blacked out again, this time from pain and shock.

It was dusk when he came back, cooler, the dreadful white of the day dissipated. It was never cold at night on the island, which assured him that he could survive the night if he could stay hidden, if he could get to cover; but he would have to wait a long time before he would have the heart to move, and meantime he had to repress his sobs at the pain in his shoulder which was now very great, as though somebody were pressing down on it with a white-hot iron. The bullet's still in there, he thought, I hope I don't get gangrene, I'm all over sand. He felt vaguely that the sand would be a disinfectant, without being able to give a reason for the idea. If I can get to the creek, he thought, I'll wash it out and perhaps I can get the bullet. It'll hurt, he thought, it'll hurt, but I can't risk an infection. Then he felt like laughing because there wasn't any chance at all of his living through this and escaping. Everybody else must be dead and there was fifteen hundred miles between him and safety.

Nevertheless he knew that he would clean his wound and try to probe it the first chance he got.

He waited and listened, surprised to hear that the oncoming quiet of night sounded just as it had last night, and the nights before that. It sounded normal, *normal,* he thought hysterically, but it did all the same. There were noises of truck motors, once he thought he heard a plane coming in but he was sure he was mistaken. The airstrip must be filled with holes, perhaps they've already cleared the seaplane anchorage, he decided, they couldn't land anything on the airstrip today, they'll have to bull-doze it over. So he waited and thought while the darkness deepened, wondering what to do. What was the point in going on, they would find him and kill him anyway, the best way would be gunfire, anyway they wouldn't torture him or any-thing, he'd make them shoot him, by struggling or running, but first he'd stay hidden as long as he could, point or no point. When it was full dark he'd get out of the emplacement some-how and get under cover, and then he'd do something, for there must be something he could do; never before in his entire life had he been in a situation that he couldn't get himself out of some way. When it was dark he'd crawl through the dunes the few hundred yards to the small creek that ran from the springs that watered the island down to the cove that formed the sea-plane anchorage. He would *do* something, something, *he* would do it. If he had to be killed, somehow or other he would make sure that he had something to do with it, he didn't want to be a mere object on a chopping block. How silly a side of beef looks hung up by the heels, how funny, just an object to be cut up and eaten, a frozen lump of stuff, like these corpses, things to be sho-velled into the sand, in the way, to be disposed of.

Now it was growing black dark, and almost cool. He put his head cautiously out to one side of Brennan's body and strained to hear. Voices all around, the island crowded with twelve thousand men, boats still coming and going from the transports anchored offshore, lots of traffic. He would work his way along the dunes and play dead whenever anybody came near. They had thought him dead once, they might do it again. He had to get out now because tomorrow they would come along and bury the dead, pushing them into a hole with a bulldozer – he didn't want to be buried alive, the thought made him shake uncontrollably as he started to work his body out from under. His left arm and shoulder felt like they were about ready to fall off. He thought he could feel the slug in his shoulder, a big solid lump of metal that he would tear out of himself. He couldn't do anything with the arm, it lay beside him like an object, a thing already dead. Maybe there isn't any blood left in it, he thought, and the notion made him sick.

When he was clear and lying on his stomach at the back of the pit he felt around in the sand until he grabbed what he was looking for, a can of rations, undented, virginal, you couldn't hurt those things with sixteen-inch artillery, let alone a grenade. He stuffed it into the front of his shirt and inch by inch crawled up the rear slope of the emplacement, stopping every few seconds to lie perfectly still. It took him almost half an hour to get to the edge.

God, it was dark. The dunes off to the right threw enormous curving shadows down on him and underneath the sand was dead black, reflecting no light. The sky wasn't so much black as empty, nothing, an interminable vault; there just didn't seem to be any light coming from anywhere. When he crawled the can of rations ground into his chest, but he had to have it. He could go thirty-six hours on what was in that can, and there would be water at the creek. Every second that passed, every inch closer to the brush and the creek improved his chances to *do something,* not to live, he wasn't going to get out of this, but to make his own will count for something.

Now he was up into the dunes and the night was moving along; it was well past midnight, he guessed, from the look of the darkness. The voices of men moving noiselessly in the sand kept on ceaselessly. They weren't combing the area but they weren't relaxing either. Once a party of half a dozen men passed over the hill of sand next to the one he was lying on. One of them seemed to have something in his hands, probably a mine detector, and from the way they spoke he could tell that they were staying pretty alert. He flattened himself on the sand, wishing he could disappear into it, then the men passed on. He couldn't hear their footfalls, they moved like ghosts across the black sand. That was the worst of the sand, somebody might trip over him in the next instant and he'd never be able to repress a cry of pain. Three hundred yards to go. He crawled faster, keeping his head down and hoping that his face reflected no light. A race was developing between him and the threatening dawn. Damn that can of food anyway, there's no place to put it.

At last he felt the ground rise, which meant that he was climbing up towards the brush and undergrowth that was barely kept alive by the creek, scrubby and sparse growth, but coloured like his clothes and plenty thick enough to hide a man. He clawed and crawled and pulled his way up the slope, seeing with fright that it was past three o'clock, and that the sky was beginning to show the first faint traces of light, dawn was under an hour away, he had to move now, and get under cover.

He fought off pain and faintness and put every thought out of his mind except the wish to see where he was headed; he was looking for the darker shadows indicating shrubs and small trees, and the intensity of his stare was justified because now he could make out the line of cover fifty yards away. He thought of running for it. His footsteps wouldn't be heard; but it was perceptibly lighter now and the movement was certain to attract attention. He could feel the oncoming light of dawn between his shoulder blades, in half an hour he'd be visible to anybody within a hundred yards or so and he was on relatively high exposed ground. Forty yards. Thirty. Getting lighter.

Then his nerve broke and wildly, unthinkingly, he stood and ran the last fifty feet in a state of mindless crazed terror, to fall full length with a crash into the branches and twigs of the first line of brush. I made it, he thought, I made it. He could see that his chances to *do something about it* had gone way way up. There were lots of things he might do now. He was hidden, well hidden, he had a little food, there was water, and the idea of water made him reckless. He half-knelt, half-stood, and pushed his way deeper into the undergrowth, down into the hollow where the creek trickled scantily through its sandy bed. He buried his face in the bitter water and wallowed again and again, up with the head and down again, water ran down into his shirt as he drank and spat and drank again.

Then he sat cross-legged, opening his shirt and splashing water on his shoulder. The sand had scrubbed his hands as he came across the dunes, so they were pretty clean, but he rubbed and cleaned them again. Then he scrubbed harshly at his shoulder, hurting himself dreadfully, but at least he was the one who was responsible. He twisted his head around to look at the wound, which had dried and been caked with sand – he tore that off and exposed the flesh, poured water on crazily; it was the only curative agent available. The water flooded the torn flesh, revealing the metal edges of the flattened slug. Every approach of his fingers to the centre of the wound was agony; a dozen times he had to make a profound act of will to be silent as he cleaned and probed with his fingers, rinsing and washing. At last by working his arm and shoulder carefully back and forth he widened the wound, inserted his fingers and grasped the metal. Then he shut his eyes, clenched his jaw, and pulled.

He had never felt anything like that before; blood spurted; the pain came in awful long pulses. But he had the lead slug in his fingers. He threw it away from him with hatred and horror and flooded his shoulder, rocking form side to side and clutching at himself. It was a long time before the flow of blood slowed and stopped. His whole left side was wet with blood and water. As he had nothing to make a bandage, he decided to move the arm and shoulder only if he absolutely had to.

He couldn't eat after that so he sat beside the water and waited for the pain to recede. There were two ways to get off the island, by plane or boat. A boat was useless, for there would be too many men aboard for him to be able to hijack it. And anyway a small boat travels too slowly to get him where he meant to go – a plane was the thing. If he could stow away aboard a small plane, he might somehow get the drop on the crew, forcing them to alter course and head for friendly waters. Very very slowly a plan began to take shape in his head, the intensity of his thinking driving the pain out of his mind.

He couldn't wait around. Every hour that he stayed on the island increased his chances of being found and killed. Today the attackers might be numbed, tired, careless; they might feel too exhausted to inspect all the hiding places – there weren't many – on the island. But by tomorrow they would be hunting him down. He wished he had a weapon of some kind, even a knife would help, and a gun would be a treasure. But he had nothing to fight with and he was weak. He would have to hide today and try to get off the island by tomorrow morning at the latest.

A plane, a plane, where would there be a plane? The airstrip was no good but there was still the anchorage. His pain was almost minimal now, considering, and he stretched out under the bank beside the water, rolling in under the clumps of reeds and grasses on the bank until he was invisible to all but the closest narrowest scrutiny. He almost relaxed; feeling began to come back to his body; a plane, a plane. Now the sun was high in the sky, lighting the underbrush, streaking it with the familiar pale greens and browns of the island vegetation. Right in front of him a frail weed of some sort straightened its spine and stood up waveringly, its leaves yellowish brown at the edges and a deeper waxy yellow in the centre, the sand grey-brown, parched whitish grasses, parchment reeds, all familiar and alive. Soon he might be able to eat something. He took his can of rations from the front of his shirt and began to open it with the attached key, hoping that the key wouldn't break off as it sometimes did, leaving the food visible but unreachable. He was careful, opening this can, more than he'd ever been at home. You just grab a can of soup and zip around it with a can-opener; of you don't get it open there's another can on the shelf. Mary had one of those wall can-openers which can hold the heaviest can in its jaws, spinning it around when you press a button. He had a sharp vision of his wife beside the kitchen cupboards, opening tomato juice cans and singing to herself.

In his can he found Spam, hard biscuit, two bars of chocolate, and a square of familiar pressed egg-like substance which he had never liked but which he now ate with thanks. He ate about a third of what was in the tin, expecting nausea at the next instant, but the food stayed down. A little later he felt stronger and revived, likely the chocolate had pepped him up.

Now, he decided, we'd better get going. He planned to work his way down the creek-bed to the mouth, where the seaplane anchorage was. He squeezed the lid on his food-pack as tight-shut as he could, shoved the thing back in his shirt, and began to wriggle along over rocks, roots, pebbles, not moving fast, going slightly downhill. He meant to spend the remaining daylight on this journey, arriving at the cove in the last of the light. He thought again of his father, his wife and children, the five of them living in quarters at the base, by now probably giving him up for dead, for they'd have heard the news. *I'm coming, Mary,* he told himself determinedly. The odds went down with every yard that he crawled. They had been millions and millions against; but now they were into the thousands and if he could hide on a plane they would be into the hundreds.

He realized suddenly, sharply, that he was being a bit light-headed and foolish, he caught himself humming tonelessly as he pushed along. He stopped humming abruptly and concentrated on keeping the reeds and grasses as still as possible as he moved. He had lots of time. He could afford to move with care. Now and then he rolled over and estimated the sun's position. He meant to arrive at the shore around six or seven o'clock. There he would eat again and settle down to watch what was going on in the anchorage.

The closer he came to the shore, the less adequate grew his cover; the brush thinned out in a straggling line and the creek widened, its course growing flatter, so that he couldn't hide in its bed. Careful, he thought, careful, don't crawl right out into the open, slide, Kelly, slide. The fall of the creek was gentle now; it didn't push behind him and hurry him along. Putting his head cautiously up the side of the bank he saw that the light penetrated his cover very freely here, the bushes were wider apart and farther from the banks, the shore very close. He began to watch very carefully as he came around each angle in the watercourse. At last, around the next bend, he caught a glimpse of open water, a small triangular corner of reflection. Could he come right to the shore? Again he crawled up the bank, and this time he knew that he was close to exhaustion, that he must eat and rest, and what he saw was not encouraging. If he went much further he would be out of the brush, completely exposed on the shore where the banks of the creek tailed off into sandy flats.

He retreated. He went back up the creek bed, regretting every inch of the fifty yards he surrendered; then he ate again and thought out his next move. There was only one way to get close enough to see what was going on. He would have to crawl right out into the water of the cove, lie at the shore line and hope to be taken for a corpse. It had worked before but he wasn't too confident this time, his luck couldn't last forever. He might not be spotted for a few minutes, half an hour at most, someone was certain to notice a body that hadn't been there before. He decided to risk it for the last quarter-hour before sunset and maybe the first few minutes of twilight – the light was trickily deceptive then. He had to see what they were doing with the planes. It had become an obsession, his will had caught and clenched tight on the idea that there would be a plane he could hijack, he was trying to create the fact by main force of desire. Meanwhile there was nothing to be done but keep under cover and watch the unassertive sun go weakly down the other side of the sky.

When the sunset had begun to shape itself in oddly dull streaks of bluish-green, he moved again, stiff, very tired, but no longer frightened, almost sure of himself, going back down to the shore. He measured his progress by the visible flattening of the banks; they pulled away from him, down and flat, exposing him, but he didn't care, he'd done all that he could with them. There was the first blackness in the east when the banks had flattened out completely, the sunset had turned a dismal metallic green, the sun was right down on the water. He lay flat where the shore met the bay, the sand under him thinned and soggy with slow ripples; he pressed his image into the unresisting sand, screwing his face into it, almost to the eyes. He let one leg float free in an inch or two of water, felt the washing play of the water in his trouser leg; in minutes the sun would be down and in the dying light he saw what he'd come all that hard hurting way to see, three reconnaissance seaplanes moored in the basin, and a fourth by the fuelling pumps. They were the kind of aircraft that a warship carries, to be catapulted free to run reconnaissance or transport missions, or gunnery spotting, to be picked up later with a derrick, just what he wanted, just the thing, he felt his heart rise and almost choke him with joy, and he let his left leg float artistically back and forth, just another dead soldier. He acted it out fiercely, nothing to investigate here, nothing to come and look at, just another harmless dead one. He heard the roar of an aero-engine as the fourth plane taxied away from the gas pump and tied up. All along the shore and all over the island lights began to come on. As the pilot left his little plane in a skiff, Johnson slid forward on his belly into about two feet of water and took off his boots; then he floated smoothly and silently out onto the calm water of the anchorage. He rolled easily over on his back and wondered how best to swim without taxing his left arm, deciding to stay on his back and use a kind of improvised frog-like kick – he mustn't splash at all – and when that position tired him, he could manage a one-armed sidestroke; he had never been able to do the crawl anyway.

Though he'd otherwise have done it in ten minutes, the short swim took half an hour, but at last he was hanging onto one of the pontoons just under the plane's door, only the small round shadow of his head out of the water. He was certainly invisible from the shore. Not even breathing hard, he hung there quietly, almost resting, treading water softly. The water was perfect for swimming, which made him want to laugh, just a nice night for a swim. He felt as though he could hang there forever.

But he had to get aboard at once. He swung in the cool water, watching and listening while the shore noises settled into a quiet night-time drone; some of the lights went off. All over the island a quiet hum of talk went up, men cooking meals, men making reports, cleaning weapons, planning the organization of the garrison. All at once Johnson felt tears in his eyes. He began to sob, not the sobs of desperate terror, but of pure human loneliness. He had the sense of not existing as a human being for any of the thousands of men whose activities comprised that giant peaceable drone. He cried quietly without shame for a long time. But when he stopped he felt new courage and purpose, and he started to get aboard the plane.

It was low-wing cabin monoplane, unarmed, no turret, no guns in the wings, a pacific and harmless plane but his salvation. He hauled himself up on the pontoon and from there clambered onto the wing, next the door. His weight made the plane rock slightly but there was no noise. Then he tried the door and it opened mercifully at his touch. As he went inside there was a sudden loud flapping noise and a splash beside the plane which made him jump. Looking down he saw a bird, not a gull but some other water bird, perched on the pontoon with its head cocked. He sighed heavily with relief. If he could have touched the bird, he'd have embraced it, a living thing that wasn't his enemy. The bird flew away in a few seconds and he bent his head and went inside.

There were seats for the pilot and two passengers, with a long narrowing space behind the seats leading to the tail which was half closed off by a fabric curtain. He scanned the instrument panel and the passenger area quickly but didn't see what he wanted, so he went to his knees and crawled past the fabric curtain into the tail. Halfway down he found a greasy bucket with rags in it, which made him remember that he had food but no water. He put the bucket carefully aside and went on with his search, running his hands into every corner of the narrowing space; it must be here; there must be something here. Something heavy or sharp, something metal; but as he worked farther along he began to despair of finding anything.

All at once he felt his heart leap as his anxiously searching palms felt something cold and hard. He clutched it and backed out of the narrow enclosure, kicking the pail along behind him, until he was out in the cabin again, where he examined his find. It was a smallish wrench, not a pipe wrench or anything like that, a tool for working on the engine most likely. It wasn't too heavy; perhaps it weighed a pound to a pound and a half. But he could strike a smart blow with it. He turned it over and over in his hands delightedly. It evened things up a little, especially since he would have the advantage of surprise.

He stuck the wrench in his belt very carefully and then got out on the wing and lowered the pail into the water. Then he took the pail back into the cabin and tried the water. It was neither fresh nor quite salt, but halfway between, just barely drinkable in an emergency but better than nothing. He decided not to use it unless he absolutely had to. He took the water and his precious wrench and crawled back into the tail, where he stretched out and settled down to wait for somebody to come. Fatigue nibbled at him; he shouldn't sleep but he was comfortable and well hidden. Drowsier and drowsier. He put out his arm and twitched the canvas curtain across the narrow passage; then he slept.

His father and Mary and the kids were in front of him, sitting at breakfast in the nook off the kitchen. The bright red Arborite top of the breakfast table gleamed cheerfully at him in the sun.

His children gabbled away to each other, happy because it was still vacation time, and his father, who was attached to Battle Group Nine Headquarters, was drinking his coffee and smiling at Mary. He couldn't catch what they were saying but they were talking about him. He wanted to speak to them, *I'm on my way, Dad. I'm coming, Mary,* and he strained to speak but couldn't make a sound. But there they were, coloured, three-dimensional, in the flesh. He rocked back and forth in an effort to make them hear, rolling on his stomach, waking as he rolled against the side of the plane, which was rocking gently as men boarded it, and it was still quite dark outside, just starting to get light. He stopped rolling and braced himself to be perfectly still. He could feel the wrench pressing against his stomach. The rocking stopped and there was a moment of quiet talk among the men up front.

With a sputter and then a roar the engine came alive, its pitch varying from loud to soft and high to low as the pilot warmed it up. Then the roar steadied and the plane taxied across the basin. Johnson had made himself the essence of stillness; he was weightless and invisible. His plan had been perfect. There couldn't possibly be more than three of them on the plane, three against one, *and they had no idea he was there,* the odds were going down very low. The plane slowed and turned, the engine revving, ready for takeoff. There was a crackling sound from the radio and the plane began to move, faster and faster, it must be damned tail-heavy, he thought, but the pilot didn't seem to notice. Maybe he was carrying extra gas, maybe he thought the passengers had put the plane a little out of trim. Then the tail came up at last, he felt himself lifted up and forward, then they were rising, off and up, up, he had never felt so *justified,* so happy. For several minutes the plane climbed and at last levelled off and set a course. It was nearly time. He would wait till they were completely at ease, and then it would be time. He peeked around the curtain.

In front of him in the passengers' seats were an army officer on the left, and on the right by the door an admiral. It had to be an admiral from the gold on his shoulder boards. Probably taking him out to the fleet, thought Johnson exuberantly, well he isn't going to get there. It was comfortably warm in the plane and they had loosened their collars and taken off their caps. Johnson tried to estimate their speed. It was a low-powered plane and would probably cruise at around a hundred and thirty to a hundred and fifty. They had been on a level course for over half an hour and allowing for wind and drift had come perhaps seventy miles. He couldn't wait till they were over the fleet. When he was sure that the plane was going to continue on a level course for some time, that the pilot was preoccupied, that the officers were relaxed and completely unsuspicious, he moved out. He saw with joy that both officers wore sidearms. He got slowly to his knees, very slowly, his system beginning to flood with adrenalin, his chest filling with outrage and hate, anger making his heart pump heavily; he moved the curtain soundlessly to one side and inched forward feeling the slow rise and fall of the floor under his knees, closer, in close, closer, the wrench clutched in his good hand.

He bounded forward with a shout of rage and smashed the admiral across the right side of the head and temple, pushing him forward and down. He raised his arm again as the other man looked back and up at him, grabbing for his gun. The second swing caught the man as he lifted his head, took him on the forehead and stunned him. As he fell back, Johnson snatched away his gun and stood nearly erect, and with an effort that hurt him very much squeezed the gun against his side with his bad arm while he hunted for the safety catch. It was in an unfamiliar place up under the trigger guard, hard to find and stiff, but he flicked it up and down a couple of times and made sure that the gun would fire. The pilot was turning his head back and forth like a robot, looking over his shoulder at Johnson and then forward at the instruments. He might have tried some trick, a roll or loop, to make Johnson fall and give the others a chance to get at him; but he didn't think of it, perhaps because of fright.

Still holding the gun under his left armpit, squeezing it against him with his bad arm, Johnson worked frantically at the handle of the cabin door – the air pressure was holding it shut – and then he found the emergency handle and the air-currents flipped the door away. The admiral was still unconscious but the other man was stirring as if trying to rise. Johnson stuck his weapon tightly in his belt, and taking care not to fall he seized the legs of the feebly moving man, ignoring the hurt in his arm, and dragged him away from the seat towards the open door. He panted and struggled, climbed across the man's body, and at last shoved him out, giving him a last push with his foot as he teetered in the door. Instantly the body vanished, whipped around behind the plane.

He did the same with the admiral's unconscious body and watched, panting and in great pain as the two black specks, miles behind the plane, curved in a long slow arc down to the water. The whole attack had taken about five minutes but to the pilot it must have seemed an endless horrifying lifetime. The odds were even now, as Johnson balanced himself against a stanchion, recovering his breath and growing aware that he was bleeding freely again. In a minute or two the sun would be up.

It's going to be a blue day, he sensed sharply, blue water, blue sky. He looked eastward while he covered the frightened pilot and counted three banks of red clouds one above the other, with blue and orange streaks of sunlight between them, a blue day. He wondered if he had done right to throw those men out; it had been done in the rage of combat and was an act of war. He hoped it was, anyway, but he was going to be a long time forgetting the sight of those plummeting unsupported black specks, live, and one of them conscious. He didn't want to have to do that again; you could get to like that kind of stuff, and if he was going to get home he didn't want to end up a murderer. Would the pilot be reasonable? he watched for a minute.

There was the incomprehensible instrument panel, and there were the foot pedals and the control column. He had no idea how to fly a plane but he knew what the various things were. He could probably steer the craft and make it rise and descend; but he didn't think he could get it down to the water safely. Would the pilot be reasonable? He shouted an order at him over the noise of the whistling slipstream.

'East, go east!' he shouted, waving his arm. The man turned and saw the motion but he did nothing and the plane stayed on course. He didn't want to have to kill the man.

'You damn fool, turn around, go east!' The pilot turned and stared back at him, keeping his hands on the control column. Johnson levelled the gun at him.

'Turn, turn,' he commanded more quietly. He was certain that the pilot understood him. The sun was over the edge of the world now, daylight rushing towards them. He waved the gun, he didn't want to do it, he didn't want to, but the pilot only shook his head and refused to obey him.

He shot the pilot three times, twice in the chest and once, dreadfully, in the face. The plane lurched to one side and he had to go up and steady the wheel, kicking and pushing with his body to dislodge the dead man. The body slumped inertly down and he sat in the pilot's position and levelled off by moving the control column gently back and then forward. He kicked out at the pilot's legs in a fit of irrational fury, they were in his way, and then swung out of his seat and pushed the body to the door and out. It bounded off a pontoon and disappeared but he didn't watch it go, he was back in his seat correcting a steep glide with great care.

When he was again on a level course he experimented with the rudder pedals. Pushing the right pedal turned the plane away from the sun towards the southwest. He pushed slowly and easily on the other, and the nose of the plane began to track round to the east, and as it came through the turn he saw that the sun was up, enormous, bright red, just up and the whole eastern sky changing colour kaleidoscopically as it climbed.

He didn't know how much fuel remained; maybe there was a reserve in the pontoons, maybe not. He might be able to stay aloft all day or only for another ten minutes, he couldn't tell. But he set a course as nearly east northeast as possible and he would hold it as long as he could. He might make friendly waters; when he came down there might be a chance to be picked up, maybe he would get home, you never can tell. But it all depended on him and his luck. It didn't depend on the enemy or anybody else.

He came back slowly on the stick. And as the bright red eye of day, the sun in the blue, went up the sky, and the bands of clouds parted in the east, he felt the drive and lift of the river of air under him, and he rose with and into the red sun, alone, absolutely unconditioned by men, and free.

Free.

Checklist

1 'A Short Walk in the Rain' was written in Hartford, Connecticut, in January 1957, and appears for the first time in this volume.

2 'A Faithful Lover' was written in Hartford, Connecticut, in January 1957, and appears for the first time in this volume.

3 'The Strategies of Hysteria' was written in Hartford, Connecticut, in February 1957, and appears for the first time in this volume.

4 'That 1950 Ford' was written in Hartford, Connecticut, in September 1957, was lightly revised in Hartford in June 1960, and appears for the first time in this volume.

5 'The World by Instalments' was written in Hartford, Connecticut, in October 1957, and appears for the first time in this volume.

6 'The Glass of Fashion' was written in Hartford, Connecticut, in November 1958, and appears for the first time in this volume.

7 'Marriage 401' was written in Hartford, Connecticut, in November 1958, and appears for the first time in this volume.

8 'The Triumph of the Liturgy' was written in Hartford, Connecticut, in December 1958, and appears for the first time in this volume.

9 'Which the Tigress, Which the Lamb?' was written in Hartford, Connecticut, in April 1959, was lightly revised in Montréal in June 1964, and appears for the first time in this volume.

10 'Presents For an Anniversary' was written in Hartford,

Connecticut, in May 1959, and appears for the first time in this volume.

11 'High Fidelity' was written in Hartford, Connecticut, in June 1960, and appears for the first time in this volume.

12 'The Regulars' was written in Hartford, Connecticut, in July 1960, and appears for the first time in this volume.

13 'From the Fields of Sleep' was written in Montréal, Québec, in August, 1961, was lightly revised in Montréal in June 1979, and appears for the first time in this volume.